ELIZABE

HAUNTINGS

THE HAUNTING OF SOPHIE BARTHOLOMEW

There was a gust of wind outside which rattled the window above the sink, sending a patter of raindrops on to the glass. And there it was. The face. It loomed towards the light of the kitchen. Gaunt, eerie, yet almost the face of a boy, wispy and faint at the edges.

The tingling spread across Sophie's head in waves. The face stared. Sophie stared back. She didn't move.

Other titles in the HAUNTINGS series:

10

ELIZABETH LINDSAY

HAUNTINGS

THE HAUNTING OF SOPHIE BARTHOLOMEW

Hippo Books
Scholastic Publications Limited
London

Scholastic Publications Ltd.,
10 Earlham Street, London WC2H 9RX, UK

Scholastic Inc.,
730 Broadway, New York, NY 10003, USA

Scholastic Tab Publications Ltd.,
123 Newkirk Road, Richmond Hill,
Ontario L4C 3G5, Canada

Ashton Scholastic Pty. Ltd.,
P O Box 579, Gosford, New South Wales,
Australia

Ashton Scholastic Ltd.,
165 Marua Road, Panmure, Auckland 6,
New Zealand

First published by Scholastic Publications Limited, 1989

Text copyright © Elizabeth Lindsay, 1989

ISBN 0 590 76045 9

For Dorothy

Chapter One

Sophie Bartholomew had an upturned nose, a pair of wide brown eyes and freckles. A shock of ginger-red hair curled about her head and bounced as she moved. Sophie Bartholomew was not popular. She was not popular because she frowned. She frowned most of the time. She squeezed her eyebrows together, wrinkled her nose and pulled the corners of her mouth down towards her chin. It made her face, which would have been a friendly face, quite ferocious. It was most off-putting and most people were put off.

Sophie's frown had become more or less permanent since Mum had made them move.

"Why can't we stay in Doon Road?" Sophie had pleaded. "I like it here."

"We can't because we can't afford it and that's that," was Mum's reply. Let's face it, Mum didn't want to move any more than Sophie did. But move they did, to a large gloomy house in Castle Street.

"Because it's cheap," said Mum.

Sophie left behind the one and only friend she had ever had, Skinny Tim Wilson, and although Mum had promised that Skinny Tim could stay in the holidays it was not the same. Sophie's frown deepened the day the van drove to Castle Street with all their things in it. Saying goodbye to Skinny Tim had been hard.

It was horrid in the new school. In the new street it was even worse. People seemed to look sideways or down their noses at Sophie and her mother.

"I don't know what's the matter with them," said Mum, exasperated. "I've never known such an unfriendly lot."

"I said we shouldn't have moved," said Sophie, her eyebrows knitting together above her nose. "Why can't we go home?" Sophie's mum sighed a big sigh and said nothing.

Sophie's mum was very nice. Everyone said so. Everyone told Sophie so, including her gran.

"She's all right," said Sophie. "But she always wants me to do things I don't want to. Like move. It's boring."

Sophie's mum was in despair. Sophie was not the sort of daughter she'd expected. Sophie didn't care – or at least, she never let on that she did. She just kept out of the way when Mum wanted to dress her in a pretty frock and dainty white shoes while she wanted to wear her old jeans and favourite green sweater with the hole in the sleeve.

"I'll wear what I like," she would snarl sitting in her new hideaway in the attic, frowning through the old skylight at a grey sky.

At her new school Sophie was soon labelled "moody boots" by her classmates, though never to her face. Sophie was fierce. Her fiercest frown was something to behold and everyone quaked before it, even Miss Pennyforth, her class teacher. Everyone except the terrible Emma Briggs, that is. In Emma's class Emma ruled. She had never spoken to Sophie. She would give her an occasional glance. The frowning redheaded newcomer interested her. But she didn't speak. Not yet. She was biding her time. So no one spoke to Sophie unless they had to and she was left alone. She didn't seem to care, or if she did she never let on.

Sophie didn't think she'd find a single friend in her new neighbourhood. Well, she didn't until one day an old black tom cat spied her trudging along the pavement on her way home from school. He slid from behind a gate and, taking a bit of a chance, rolled on his back in front of her, wriggling his legs in the air. What an invitation! Sophie stopped. She looked at the cat. She looked up the street and down the street. No one in sight. She knelt down.

"Want your tummy tickled?"

The cat stretched, his eyes fixed encouragingly on hers. Before she knew it Sophie found her hand caressing the soft downy fur of the cat's tummy. The cat purred and as he purred interesting things happened to Sophie's face. Her mouth relaxed. Her eyes opened and the lines on her forehead disappeared. She began to smile, stretching her freckles upwards until she looked like a different person.

"Hello, dear. I see you met Mr Spiv," said a voice from above her head.

In an instant the frown was back and Sophie stood up quickly to see who it was. She found herself looking into the face of a wrinkled old lady whose steel-grey hair was curly like her own though there was not so much of it. The old lady ignored the frown or perhaps didn't see it, for she added, "I'm Mrs Russett. I live here at number nine. Won't you come in and meet the others?" Mrs Russett pulled the gate open and Sophie, in spite of herself, went in.

The inside of Mrs Russett's house was shabby. It hadn't seen a lick of paint in years. Sophie stood awkwardly in the hallway.

"This way," said Mrs Russett, leading Sophie into the back room. It was quite a clutter of chairs, tables, cushions and cats. Mr Spiv trotted in behind them, jumped on to the table and paced up and down hoping for more strokes.

"Mr Spiv you've already met," said Mrs Russett. "This is Esmeralda and that's her cushion. The one she's on. If you want to you can tickle her ears." Esmeralda, being somewhat temperamental, could only be stroked if she was sitting comfortably. She never even went out in the wet.

"A blessed nuisance she is," said Mrs Russett fondly. "Still, there you are. Cats is cats. And this is Gerty. Come on, Gerty! Come and say hello."

The fluffiest cat Sophie had ever seen jumped from the windowsill and padded across the floor to greet them. The nicest thing was that her coat was the same colour as Sophie's hair.

"She looks like she's wearing ginger pantaloons," said Sophie. Her eyes lit up and she forgot to frown. Mrs Russett looked pleased.

"Gerty is a most unusual cat. Being female and being ginger an' all. Just like you. Won't you tell us your name, ducks?"

"It's Sophie."

4

"Well, there can't be much wrong with you. The cats are pleased to see you. Animals always know, especially cats. Canny creatures are cats. That's why I like 'em."

Gerty rubbed herself against Sophie's legs.

"Oh, she does like you. Want to brush her?" asked Mrs Russett.

"Can I?"

"She loves it. Here's the brush."

Gerty certainly did love it. She pulled herself across the floor, purring delightedly at every brush stroke.

"I love Gerty," said Sophie, her frown completely gone and a beaming smile on her face.

"I know what you mean," said Mrs Russett. "Have a toffee, Sophie."

In an instant, Mrs Russett knew what few people realized – underneath that frown Sophie was lonely. Mrs Russett's heart went out to her.

"I've got to go now. Mum'll wonder where I am," said Sophie, her mouth bulging with treacle toffee.

"Come and see us again soon, Sophie. Don't leave it too long, ducks," said Mrs Russett. "You're only at number thirteen after all."

"She knows where I live," thought Sophie, surprised.

Mrs Russett gave a cheery wave from the gate, wearing Gerty draped over her shoulders like a furry ginger shawl. Sophie smiled, her frown gone and forgotten as she waved back.

As she opened the door to her house the yellow one and three on the cracked green paint seemed to glow. Sophie stared at the numbers.

"Silly. How can they glow?" she thought. She touched the one and took her finger away sharply. A tingling sensation ran all the way up her arm. She shook her hand.

"Ouch!" she said. "Must be electric."

"Take your shoes off and put your slippers on, Sophie. I've washed the hall floor," shouted Mum from the kitchen. In a moment the frown was back. Sophie banged about, one shoe went here, one there and her feet started to get cold because she couldn't find her slippers.

"I bet Mrs Russett never bothers about dirty shoes. She's got cats with dirty feet going everywhere."

Upstairs in her room Sophie got out writing paper, sat at her table and began a letter to Skinny Tim.

13 Castle Street
Snareswick
SN1 4MW

Dear Skinny Tim,

Castle Street is horrid because no one ever speaks to us and Snareswick rotten school is even worse. It is full of stuck-up little rats. I am thinking of running away. One nice thing. There is an old lady called Mrs Russett at number nine. She has three cats. One is called Gerty and has the same colour hair as me. She has to be brushed lots. Mrs Russett gave me treacle toffee. I have still got a bit stuck to my front tooth. I hope the tooth doesn't go bad. But it will be worth it. The toffee is the best I have ever tasted. Perhaps I won't run away after all.

Love,

Sophie

Mum's voice echoed up the stairs.

"Tea's ready."

A delicious smell of toast wafted up. Mum had left the kitchen door open. Light from the kitchen fell into the hall. Sophie looked between the banister rails. It was getting dark. Gloom spread into the rest of the house, making the kitchen seem more inviting.

"I'll post my letter tomorrow on the way to school," she thought. "That is, if Mum's got a stamp. What a dump! Maybe I will run away after all. Nothing exciting's going to happen here."

Sophie's frown deepened. Then, suddenly and unexpectedly out of the gloom, came a terrific crash. In the kitchen Mum screamed and Sophie ran as fast as her legs could take her to find out what had happened. Mum had dropped a saucepan of baked beans on to another saucepan in the sink. Tomato sauce had splattered up the wall. But what was odd was that Mum seemed frozen to the spot. Her mouth was open and fixed, her eyes staring at the kitchen window.

"What's up?" asked Sophie.

As if coming out of a dream, Mum mumbled, "I saw a face. At the window."

"What sort of face?"

"It was horrible."

"Oh, yeah? How horrible?"

"Just horrible."

"Well, I bet there's no one there," said Sophie. She wrenched back the bolt on the back door and opened it. It was almost dark outside and just starting to drizzle.

"Told you. No one there. Must have been your imagination, Mum."

"Yes, must have been," said Mum, who was still

dazed. Sophie, in a burst of generosity and because she was feeling quite hungry, said, "You sit down, Mum, I'll dish up."

Gratefully Mum sat down. Sophie devoured her baked beans. Mum didn't touch hers.

"Odd," thought Sophie, and it was. It was the second odd thing to happen. The first, she remembered, was the electric shock she got from the number on the front door.

"Very odd," said Sophie to herself later that night as she lay in bed mulling things over. Tomorrow she was going to give the front door a good going over to see if it had any wires or funny things attached.

"Yes, that's what I'll do first thing," she thought as she dropped off to sleep.

Chapter Two

"Sophie! Sophie, will you get up? I'm not telling you again!" It was Mum shouting up the stairs. Sophie opened her eyes and screwed up her face. She could feel the cold on her nose. In bed it was cosy and warm. She closed her eyes.

"Sophie!"

The voice was cross. Sophie opened her eyes and looked at the clock. Ten to eight. She was late. She remembered there was something she wanted to do. Something interesting. What was it? The front door! She was going to check it for wires. All of a tumble, Sophie clambered out of bed and ran for the bathroom. It was a bit warmer in there. Mum had left the electrical wall heater on.

"This house is a fridge and I don't like freezing," Sophie grumbled. "Why can't we have central heating like everybody else?"

"Don't forget to turn the heater off!" called Mum as Sophie charged for her bedroom.

"Oh, drat it!"

Sophie ran back to the bathroom, jumped at the heater string and pulled hard. The heater switched off but the string came away in her hand.

"Oh, no! Now I'm for it!"

When Sophie finally arrived downstairs she put the heater string on the kitchen table next to her bowl of tepid porridge.

"How did you manage that?" asked Mum, her face frosty.

"I only pulled it." Mum sighed.

"Eat your porridge. I don't want to be late for work again this morning. Mr Smart was shirty yesterday when I missed the bus."

Sophie put a spoonful of the cool porridge in her mouth. Her frown established itself for the day.

"Must you frown like that, Sophie? You're getting lines. It's ridiculous at your age."

"I can't help the way my face goes."

"Try smiling," said Mum.

"What? And eat porridge at the same time? It's enough to make you sick."

Mum gave up. She put Sophie's packed lunch ready on the table.

"Can we have a cat, Mum?"

"No, we can't."

"Do I have to finish this?"

"If you'd got up when I first called it would have been perfectly edible."

"If we had a cat it would finish up things like porridge," said Sophie.

"No," said Mum again. Sophie gave up.

As they put their coats on Sophie eyed the front door. She really wanted to give it the once over right away and was cross with herself for not having woken up early as she had planned.

"I'm working late tonight," said Mum. "Got your key?"

Sophie nodded.

"Your tea's in the oven. It'll take twenty minutes. There's some salad in the fridge."

"I don't know why we have the fridge on. We don't need to. This house is freezing."

"Oh, Sophie! Just hurry up."

Mum opened the front door. Sophie eyed the tattily painted thirteen. She was about to touch the three when Mum gave her a push.

"Hurry up. Whatever's the matter with you? We haven't got all day."

Mum dragged the reluctant Sophie along the pavement. Sophie was fed up. But she comforted herself with the thought that she'd have something interesting to do when she got home and, better still, Mum wouldn't be there to stop her from doing it.

They passed number nine. Mrs Russett was on the doorstep talking to the postman.

"Hello, Sophie!" said Mrs Russett. Sophie grinned. "Bring your mum in to say hello when you've got time."

Mum half-turned, surprised by such friendliness, but didn't stop. There was no time. Mum was frightened of Mr Smart. She didn't want to get on the wrong side of him. She didn't want the sack.

"I will!" called Sophie.

The bus was standing at the bus stop when they turned into the main road. They had to run. The last person at the stop saw them coming and took a long time getting on so the bus had to wait.

"That was kind, dear," said Mum, all of a puff. "Thank you."

The person looked at Mum then looked at Sophie. Sophie's frown deepened. She didn't know where to look. The person was Emma Briggs.

The bus was crowded so they had to stand. As the bus swayed and lurched Sophie's elbow kept knocking Emma's school bag. She wished it wouldn't but she couldn't help it. The bus came to a sudden stop. Sophie banged into Emma.

"Sorry," said Sophie. Emma turned round and faced her. She didn't say anything.

"For knocking into you," said Sophie. Emma looked.

" 'S'all right," she said at last. Sophie felt herself go red. Her face flamed. That made her cross with herself. The next stop was Mum's.

"You have got your door key?" Mum asked. Sophie nodded. "See you tonight then."

Mum got off and walked quickly between the people on the pavement. Emma's gaze followed her until she was out of sight.

"Your mum?" she asked. Sophie nodded again.

"She looks nice." Sophie's face relaxed a little. "But tired."

Sophie thought about that as the bus moved off. She tried to spot Mum amongst the hurrying people. Were they all late for work? she wondered. Emma was right. Mum was nice and she was tired.

"I shall try and be nice too," she promised herself. Her frown deepened as she concentrated. "Nice like Mrs Russett." She remembered Mrs Russett waving goodbye with Gerty wrapped around her shoulders.

"Have you got a cat?" she asked Emma.

"Yes. Have you?" Sophie shook her head.

"She sleeps on my bed," said Emma. "On the pillow next to my nose actually."

"Really?" said Sophie impressed. "What's her name?"

"Fluff," said Emma. "Fluff the Puff. Because she's like a powder puff."

"There's a lady in our road called Mrs Russett and she's got a fluffy cat called Gerty," said Sophie.

"What colour?" said Emma.

"Ginger. Same as me." Sophie grinned. She had forgotten her shyness. "What colour's yours?"

"Grey," said Emma. "With orange eyes."

"How lovely!" said Sophie, going all dreamy at the thought.

Emma grinned, taking in Sophie without her face set in a frown. Maybe this Sophie girl is all right, she thought. But she wasn't going to commit herself to friendship. Not yet.

When they jumped from the bus Emma was claimed immediately by several girls from Sophie's class. A couple of boys walked at a respectful distance and Sophie felt herself melt into the background. She re-established her frown and slid into the school playground, keeping herself well back from the throng that surrounded Emma. She spent the day as disdainfully as usual, locked into her friendless isolation, hell bent on keeping the world away with her ferocious glare.

So Sophie was surprised when someone spoke her name at the bus stop on the way home. It was Emma.

"Oh, hello!" said Sophie. The two girls at Emma's shoulder, as if receiving a silent command, moved away and they stood alone.

"You live in the next street to me," said Emma.

"Do I?"

13

"Castle Street. I asked." Sophie was touched by Emma's curiosity. So much so that she volunteered more information.

"Yes, number thirteen." Emma's eyes widened.

"Number thirteen," she said. "But that's . . ."

It seemed as if she was going to say something else but changed her mind. "That's been empty for years."

"It feels like it," said Sophie. "It's like living in an iceberg. I hope it gets warmer in the summer."

"What's the house like?"

Sophie felt the question was important to Emma but didn't quite know what she wanted to hear.

"It's . . . it's all right. A bit gloomy. Cold of course. But I don't care. I just wish we'd never moved, that's all."

Emma paused. Sophie sensed that she couldn't tell Emma whatever it was she wanted to know. At least, not at the moment. The question would need to be more direct. She would wait. Emma would ask it sooner or later, she thought. In the meantime she was flattered to be the centre of Emma's attention. After all, Emma had loads of friends and had chosen to talk to her.

On the bus ride home Emma asked her more questions about herself. Did she have any brothers and sisters? What did her mum do? What did her dad do? A difficult question for Sophie to answer. What should she say? She decided she liked Emma and would trust her. She explained that she didn't know her dad. That he had gone before she was born and that Mum wouldn't talk about him. Emma didn't ask any more questions after that. For a while she was silent. At last she said,

"That's tough. My dad drives me up the wall but I

like him. He's like a teddy bear when he's in a good mood. It must be horrid not having one."

This burst of sympathy caught Sophie unawares. A lump came into her throat and tears pricked at her eyes. She looked out of the window and thought, my dad can't have been very nice. Not if he left Mum with me on the way. She swallowed her tears and said in a wobbly voice,

"My mum's great. She works hard to keep us both. And I've got a gran, an' all."

"Yeah," said Emma. "I can see how just having a mum and no brothers and sisters could have its advantages."

"Have you got brothers and sisters?"

"One brother and one sister. It can be a drag," said Emma.

Sophie wondered how on earth it could be a drag. Someone to talk to, to share secrets with, to have fun with . . . She'd always wanted a sister.

"Still, I don't let them get in the way," said Emma.

The bus pulled into the kerb at the bus stop. They stepped on to the pavement. Sophie felt in her pocket for her front door key. It wasn't there. She felt in her other pocket. No key. Then she remembered. She'd emptied all her pockets looking for her old-fashioned threepenny bit. The key with all her other bits and bobs was sitting on her dressing table.

Sophie's face was a picture of dismay. "What's the matter?" Emma asked.

"I left my door key in my room," she said. "That means I can't get in till mum gets back."

"You said you'd got it when your mum asked."

The accusation took Sophie aback. Then she remembered Mum asking her on the bus that morning if she had her key.

"I thought I had." Sophie brightened. "I know, I'll ask Mrs Russett if I can stop at her house till Mum gets back."

"No," said Emma. "Don't do that. Come back with me. My mum won't mind."

"Oh, no," said Sophie. "No, I couldn't do that."

"Why not?"

Sophie felt overwhelmed with shyness at the thought of meeting Emma's brother and sister and mum and dad. She fumbled for an excuse.

"Well, I . . . Mum would be worried if she came back and I wasn't there."

"That's all right," said Emma. "We can go down Castle Street and leave her a note. Come on."

Sophie followed her behind, her feet dragging as she tried to gain control of her feelings. When Emma made a decision she certainly expected it to be obeyed.

"Do I want to go or don't I?" Sophie came to a halt. She noticed the fine October drizzle speckling her coat sleeve. The raw chill made her shiver.

"Come on!" called Emma. "Before we get soaked." She beckoned with an exaggerated wave. Sophie smiled.

"I'm coming!" she called.

The note, by the time they had written it, was rather damp.

"Here," said Emma. "Put it through the letter-box."

The tatty thirteen was barely visible in the gloom as Sophie pushed the note through the letter box. Gingerly she touched the three. Nothing. She traced over it with her finger. Nothing at all. All in my imagination, she sighed.

"Hurry up!" said Emma. She was impatient to be

gone. Her voice had an urgency in it that suprised Sophie. Not wanting to keep Emma waiting she turned. From inside the house came a kind of hissing noise. Sophie looked back. The tatty thirteen glowed briefly in the twilight and someone somewhere seemed to laugh.

"Did you see that, Emma?"

"See what?" said Emma, edging her way down the pavement.

"Oh, nothing. I just thought . . ." Sophie trailed off. Was it her imagination or had something happened? Emma, beside herself to be gone, grabbed Sophie's arm.

"Come on," Emma said. "It's raining."

But Sophie knew that wasn't the reason she wanted to go. Emma's face was pale under the street light. Emma Briggs was scared. But scared of what? Something was going on that she, Sophie, didn't know about. But whatever it was was not going to remain a mystery for long. Not if she, Sophie Bartholomew, had anything to do with it.

Chapter Three

Emma's brother Simon let them in. The warmth of the house burst on to the doorstep to greet them.

"Mum!" called Emma. "Mum! I've brought a friend home." There were a few moments of silence until a door opened upstairs. Mrs Briggs came downstairs to the hall.

"Hello," she said and smiled.

"This is Sophie Bartholomew. She's lost her door key and can't get in till her mum gets home."

Sophie noticed the slight untruth. It was no good.

"I didn't actually lose it, Mrs Briggs, I forgot it."

"Oh dear!" said Mrs Briggs. "How trying for you. Come in and meet the others. Emma'll get you some tea. You'll have to excuse me, I'm finishing some work in the study. But welcome, welcome. I'll see you later." Her voice trailed off as she went back upstairs, smiling vaguely, her mind with her work.

Emma led the way to the kitchen. Sophie followed. Simon followed Sophie, eyeing her with a kind of caution. In the kitchen was Emma's little sister Hannah, and Anne-Marie, who was French, feeding Hannah a boiled egg.

"This is Sophie," said Emma.

Hannah spat a bread crust at her by way of greeting and wiped sticky egg-covered fingers across the table.

"Hannah, please no!" said Anne-Marie.

"I'm Simon," said Simon. He half-smiled at Sophie, unsure of her response.

"I'm pleased to meet you," said Sophie politely.

Emma paused a moment, recognizing Sophie's shyness.

"We all drive Anne-Marie mad but she doesn't mind," Emma said.

"I mind," said Anne-Marie. "Please, do sit, Sophie." Sophie sat. "Oh, no, first take off your coat, please."

Sophie stood up and took off her soggy coat. As no one offered to take it she hung it over the back of her chair and sat down again.

"Want something to eat?" Emma asked.

"My tea's in the oven. I must eat it when I get home," she said.

"Have a snack then. What we got, Anne-Marie?"

"Don't ask me. I have no ideas."

"We could open a tin of tuna fish and make tuna fish sandwiches," suggested Simon.

"Do you like tuna fish?" said Emma. Sophie nodded.

"Yes, lovely."

They put the sandwiches on a big plate and took them upstairs to Emma's room. Simon came too. Sophie thought Emma was going to tell him to go away but she didn't. She gave a sort of resigned sigh. Sophie was glad Simon was there. Although they'd hardly spoken she liked him.

They sat silently munching until Simon said, through a mouthful, "Do you live close by?" Sophie nodded.

"In Castle Street."

"Number thirteen," said Emma as if this was significant. Simon's eyes widened.

"Number thirteen!"

Sophie stopped chewing. A tingling sensation ran from the bottom of her spine to the top and spread across her head like the pricking of little needles.

"The ghost house!" Simon sat back on his heels. "Whew!"

They both stared at Sophie, waiting for her reaction. Did that explain the funny number thirteen and the face at the kitchen window? What about her threepenny bit? She thought she had lost it but maybe a ghost had stolen it. As she reviewed things she finished chewing and swallowed her mouthful. The others looked at her expectantly.

"Who says it's a ghost house?"

"Everyone," said Simon. "It's famous."

"Famous for what?"

"For hauntings."

They waited for Sophie to take in what was obviously news to her. They watched as she prodded a sandwich across the plate.

"Is that why it was empty for so long?"

"Must have been," Emma said. Suddenly Sophie was angry.

"And they never said anything to my mum. She was half scared to death the other night."

"What happened?" They both wanted to know.

"And Mrs Russett never said anything either."

"What happened the other night?" said Emma insistently.

"They say people have been driven mad living there," said Simon. His eyes were wide. "No one stays for long. That's true, isn't it, Em?"

"Of all the cheek! Of all the cheek!" said Sophie. "And now everyone's waiting to see what'll happen to us."

Her face, which had relaxed, took on its frown and glowered. She clenched her fists and hit the floor with a violence that made the sandwich plate jump.

"Well, nothing will. Nothing at all. I'm not afraid of ghosts. Never have been, never will be."

"We could be ghost hunters," said Emma.

Simon, who'd been holding his breath, let it out slowly through his teeth. As he did so the tension in Sophie melted.

"My mum saw a face outside the kitchen window last night. She said it was horrible. When I opened the back door it was gone. It was so horrible mum went all funny and had to sit down."

"Cor!" said Simon.

"And something else." She paused.

"What else?" said Emma.

"The thirteen on the front door glows. Only sometimes. It did it just now. When we put the note through the letter box. And there was a hissing and a sort of laugh. And last night it gave me a kind of electric shock when I touched it."

Emma and Simon sat waiting but Sophie didn't say any more. At last Simon said, "And you weren't scared, honestly?"

"Honestly," said Sophie. "I don't know why not but I wasn't and I'm not scared now."

"I am," Simon shuddered. "How about you,

21

Em?" Emma looked at the floor.

"Yes," she said. "It *is* scary."

The three of them sat lost in their own thoughts for a moment. It was Simon who broke the silence.

"*Could* we be ghost hunters?" he said.

"Well," said Sophie, "we could if we knew what we were hunting. Nobody speaks to us in our street. So nobody's said what the ghosts are."

"Bangs in the night? Bumps on the stairs?" suggested Emma.

"Nothing like that so far," said Sophie, "but we haven't been there long."

"Is it creepy? The house, I mean," said Simon.

"Gloomy. I call it gloomy but you might call it creepy," said Sophie. "Why don't you come round? Mum won't mind as long as you wipe your feet."

Simon looked willing and unwilling at the same time. Emma made the decision.

"All right," she said. "We will." Simon swallowed.

"Come tomorrow," said Sophie. "It's Saturday. When I get home tonight I'm going to look for wires on the door. Tomorrow I'm going to ask Mrs Russett about the ghosts."

Sophie stood up. Crumbs fell from her skirt to the floor. Out of habit she stooped to pick them up.

"Don't bother," said Emma. "They'll get hoovered when Mrs Peters comes."

It was no use. Sophie didn't feel right leaving them. Mum would've been cross. She gathered them carefully and shook them on to the plate.

"Thanks very much for the sandwiches," she said. "Very nice." Emma didn't say anything.

"You're welcome," said Simon. He smiled an open, wide smile. The front doorbell rang.

"Go on, Simon. See who it is," said Emma. Simon,

still with his smile, nipped downstairs.

There was an uneasy pause. To fill it Sophie said, "You are lucky to have a brother."

"Yes," said Emma, realizing how fortunate she was altogether. "Yes, I'm very lucky." She smiled. The smile reassured Sophie and the unease she had felt vanished.

"Tomorrow, then," said Emma. "Tomorrow morning."

There were feet on the stairs and Simon poked his head around the door.

"It's your mum, Sophie," he said, and by way of a warning, "She looks a bit out of sorts."

Sophie sprang to the door and hurried downstairs. Mum stood awkward and damp in the hall.

"Oh, there you are, Sophie. I hope you haven't been a nuisance."

The study door on the landing opened and Mrs Briggs followed Sophie and Emma downstairs.

"I'm so sorry about Sophie," said Mum. "I asked I don't know how many times if she'd got her key."

"I thought I had, Mum."

"Oh, good lord! It's been nice to meet her. I'm Helen Briggs by the way," said Mrs Briggs.

"I'm pleased to meet you, I'm sure. My name's Ann. Ann Bartholomew."

"Won't you stop to have a cup of tea?"

"Oh, no. I couldn't put you to the trouble."

"No trouble. I hope you fed Sophie well, Emma?"

"Tuna fish sandwiches," said Emma, her gaze on Sophie's mum.

"Simon, ask Anne-Marie to put the kettle on. Let me take your coat, Ann. It's soaked. Here, Emma, hang it up for me then scoot you two. Come into the front room, Ann, and warm up. It's a dreadful night."

Sophie watched amazed as Mum allowed herself to be ushered out of her coat and into the front room. People did what Emma wanted, she knew, but it seemed they also did what Emma's mum wanted.

Emma hung the coat on the coat rack.

"Come on," she said. "I'll show you my posters."

It was quite late when they got home. Sophie was feeling tired. She looked at the tatty thirteen as Mum closed the door and glanced around for wires when Mum put on the light.

"Wipe your feet," Mum said. Sophie did it automatically. Mum didn't bother to check. She hung up her soggy coat and headed for the kitchen.

"Food and then bed," she said. "If the dinner's still edible."

It was sort of. It was a vegetable and oat bake. When Mum got it out of the oven and put it on the table Sophie could see that the top had a hard crust on it and the sides were glued to the dish.

"Never mind," said Mum. "We can eat the middle."

Normally she would have been cross at such a disaster but she seemed quite cheerful.

"Emma seems a nice girl," she said. She handed Sophie a plate of overcooked bake.

"She's in my class."

"Well, I thought her mum a dear."

"Did you?"

"A very nice woman. She says you can go round whenever you like, Sophie. Very warm and open. Really nice."

Sophie mulled over the events of the day as she chewed and dutifully swallowed her overcooked food. She had made friends with Emma Briggs. The famous Emma from whom she had learned that she and Mum were living in a haunted house. It was rather odd. What had felt ordinary and normal this morning had suddenly become something quite different.

"Would you like some more?" Mum asked. "I can scrape some off the bottom."

"No thanks. I've had tuna fish sandwiches, don't forget."

"I'll put this dish to soak and do the washing-up then."

Sophie felt a sudden tingling run up her spine. The same tingling as at Emma's house.

"No," she said. "Don't. I'll do it."

"It's late, Sophie. You're tired."

"No, I want to, please."

Mum, surprised, gave in. After all it was Friday. Saturday tomorrow. No school. No work. She picked up a newspaper she'd left lying on the table and flicked idly through the pages. Sophie took the plates to the sink.

There was a gust of wind outside which rattled the window above the sink, sending a patter of raindrops on to the glass. And there it was. The face. It loomed towards the light of the kitchen. Gaunt, eerie, yet almost the face of a boy, wispy and faint at the edges. The tingling spread across Sophie's head in waves. The face stared. Sophie stared back. She didn't move. The tingling stopped. Without giving it a thought Sophie put her hands to her head, wriggled her fingers and poked her tongue out. Then she danced in front of the sink

25

pulling the worst face she could manage.

"Yeah, yeah, yeah, yeah, yeah!" she cried.

The whatever it was that was looking in melted away.

"Sophie, what on earth are you doing?" said Mum as Sophie wrenched back the bolt and opened the back door.

"Just seeing if it's raining," she said.

There was nothing outside. Nothing at all. Just the chill wetness of a cold October night. Sophie came back indoors.

"Well, at least I've seen it," she thought. "I'll be able to tell the others in the morning."

She bolted the door and went back to the washing-up.

"Of course it's raining," said Mum. "It's been raining all evening. Sometimes I think I've a lunatic for a daughter. I don't know. I really don't."

Mum kissed Sophie goodnight on the landing. She was tired. Sophie could see dark rings under her eyes.

"If only she didn't make such a fuss about things that don't matter," Sophie thought.

"Mum! Have a hug."

Sophie gave Mum a long squeeze. Mum put her hand on Sophie's curls.

"Night, night, love," she said.

Sophie lay in bed listening to the rain and listening for sounds which weren't the rain. She didn't hear anything that wasn't the wind or the tapping of the plane tree on her window.

"How do hauntings begin?" she wondered. "I wish I knew." But she didn't wonder for long as she fell asleep.

Chapter Four

By morning the rain had stopped. A glimmer of weak sun crept between the gaps in the curtains and fell on Sophie's frayed red-brown carpet. She wondered what time it was. Had she overslept? No. When she looked at her watch it said half past eight. It wasn't early but it wasn't late either. She swung her legs out of bed, feeling the chill of the room grab at her. She pulled on her dressing gown, fumbled for her slippers and went downstairs.

There was a letter lying on the doormat. She picked it up and took it to the kitchen with her. It was addressed to Mum. She put it on the table. She filled the kettle and lit the gas. She looked through the window into the overgrown garden. Nothing there.

"What a gloomy dump!" she thought. She switched on the light. "That's better."

She stretched, then huddled near the gas cooker for warmth.

When the kettle boiled she made tea. She poured

out two mugfuls, put the letter between her teeth and carried the mugs carefully upstairs. She pushed open Mum's bedroom door with her knee.

Mum was still asleep when she went in. She opened her eyes when Sophie put the cups on the rickety bedside table.

"That *is* kind," Mum said.

"Shall I pull the curtains? The sun's trying to shine."

"Yes. Then get in here with me. You must be freezing."

Sophie's feet were chilled and her fingers, in spite of carrying two mugs of tea, were blue.

"There's a letter," said Sophie. She wriggled into Mum's bed. It was wonderfully warm. She put a foot on Mum's leg. Mum gasped with the shock.

"My goodness, Sophie! You *are* cold. Did you put the heater on in the bathroom?"

"No, I forgot."

"Never mind. Let's see who the letter's from."

Sophie sipped her steaming tea. The writing on the envelope looked familiar.

"It's from Gran," said Mum, before she'd even opened it. "I expect she wants to come and stay."

"Oh, no!" thought Sophie, knitting her eyebrows together. "Not Gran!"

"Does she have to?" she said out loud.

"Don't be difficult, Sophie. Let's see what she says." Mum began reading the letter.

"Read it out loud," said Sophie. Mum cleared her throat.

"Dear Ann, Your letter came yesterday. Glad to hear you're both settling in O.K. Have taken some time off work. Thought I could pack a suitcase tomorrow and come over on Saturday. If not convenient ring Mrs Evans next door before ten o'clock Saturday."

"What's the time?" Sophie said.

"Mind your tea, Sophie."

"If we got up now we could ring and stop her from coming."

Mum ignored this and went on.

"I shall come by bus to Snareswick. Send Sophie to meet me. She can carry my suitcase. See you Saturday. Love, Mum."

"What a cheek! I'm not carrying her rotten suitcase," said Sophie. "I've got other things to do."

"The trouble is she doesn't say what time she's getting here," said Mum. "Never mind. We'll get her room ready and both go to the bus station this afternoon." Sophie frowned.

"Mum, I've got things to do. I've got Emma and Simon coming round." Mum looked at the frown, sighed and relented.

"All right, I'll go and meet her by myself. But she is your gran, Sophie. She'd like it if you were there to meet her."

"She wants a slave for a grand-daughter. It was awful last time she stayed. It was do this and do that. And she wanted to cut my hair."

"She wanted you to look nice."

"There's nice and nice. My nice is not her nice," said Sophie. She jumped out of bed. "I'm getting up."

By the time they had finished breakfast it was ten o'clock. It was quite warm in the kitchen but what would Emma and Simon feel about the rest of the house? It was freezing.

"They'll have to keep their coats on," Sophie decided.

Mum piled the breakfast dishes into the sink.

"Do you think Gran'll like the room at the back that looks over the garden?" she said. "It's got that little fireplace in it. We could light a fire and make it cosy for her."

"We haven't got any coal," said Sophie.

"We can buy some."

"I expect she'll freeze just like we do and moan about it a lot," said Sophie.

"Yes," said Mum. "She does feel the cold."

"Haven't you told her we're living in a fridge? If you ring Mrs Evans now you could get Gran before she leaves. I bet she wouldn't come if she knew how cold it is. Shall I ring?"

"I want her to come, Sophie. We'll just have to make sure she isn't cold. I want her to come because . . ." Mum trailed off. ". . . because I want someone to talk to."

Sophie looked at Mum. She still had the bags under her eyes and she looked sad. Sophie went tight inside with a kind of ache.

"I can talk to you, Mum."

"I know you can, Sophie. You do, love. But, well . . . it'd be nice to talk to Mum too. She won't stay long, I don't expect. Let's make her stay as nice as possible, eh?"

Sophie gave in. She would try. She nodded.

"All right, Mum. Shall I go and buy a bag of coal? They've got some at the corner shop."

"If you think you can carry it," said Mum.

Sophie looked at Mum and narrowed her eyes. Did she think she was some kind of weakling or something? Of course she could carry it! She set off for the shop with Mum's purse in her pocket.

The bag of coal was much heavier than Sophie expected. By the time she got to Mrs Russett's gate she had to stop. She let the bag slither to the pavement with a scrunch. Sophie was hot. Her arms ached. Something furry twisted itself around Sophie's ankle and brushed itself against the coal sack. It was Mr Spiv.

"Hello," said Sophie. She ran her hand along his furry back and scratched him behind the ear. Mr Spiv leaned in to her fingers appreciatively and purred.

"It's no good. I've got to get the coal home but I'll come back and see you later," she said.

Sophie lifted the coal sack with difficulty. Somehow her aching arms managed to carry it to the doorstep of number thirteen. She stood wondering how to open the door without putting down the sack when two hands gripped her round the waist and squeezed. This took her completely by surprise and she dropped the sack of coal, which split at the top, spilling lumps of dusty coal across the doorstep. Angrily, Sophie turned round. There was no one there. Only a faint hissing and the sound of a distant laugh.

"I'll get you for that!" Sophie muttered. "You see if I don't. Nobody meddles with Sophie Bartholomew and gets away with it. Especially cowardy, cowardy custards who run away."

The front door opened. Mum looked at the mess on the ground.

"I'm sorry Mum. I dropped the bag. It burst."

"So I see," said Mum. "I've found a coal scuttle.

I'll fetch it."

"I'll put it in the coal scuttle," said Sophie when Mum came back. "It was my fault." Bits of coal seemed to have bounced everywhere.

"You'll have to come in and clean up when you've finished," said Mum. "If you put coal dust finger-prints on anything I'll be furious."

"I won't, I promise!" Sophie began to drop bits of coal into the scuttle. They pinged noisily against the metal.

"Hello, Sophie dear." It was Mrs Russett. "Mr Spiv said he'd seen you."

"Hello," said Sophie. It came to her that perhaps Mrs Russett was a little mad. After all cats can't talk. "The bag burst," she said.

"What a shame!" said Mrs Russett.

The furry collar around Mrs Russett's coat moved. It was Gerty. Sophie smiled.

"Hello, Gerty."

Gerty stretched a paw towards Sophie in a friendly catlike way. Sophie came up to Mrs Russett and nuzzled Gerty with her nose. Mrs Russett chuckled. "She likes that."

"I don't want her to get covered in coal dust," said Sophie. "But I wish I could stroke her."

"You are with your nose," said Mrs Russett.

Sophie was pleased Gerty liked her.

"I've got some friends coming round soon," she said. "Can I bring them to meet you?"

"I'd like that," said Mrs Russett. "And the cats would too. Friends coming round. How nice!"

Mrs Russett left Sophie to finish picking up the coal. If friends were coming round there were one or two things she wanted to do.

At last Gran's room was ready. There was coal in the coal scuttle. Sophie had found some kindling sticks in the garden which she hoped would dry out in time. Matches and newspapers were all ready too. The room was cleaned and the bed made up with two hot-water bottles in it.

"It's all done," said Mum, flushed from her efforts. "You can go and play now."

Sophie went to her room to check she had made her bed. She had another quick look for her threepenny bit and found her letter to Skinny Tim on the floor. She hadn't even got as far as putting it in an envelope.

"There's a lot more to write now. I can tell him about the hauntings. And about being grabbed from behind. Who did that? That's what I want to know."

There was a loud knock on the front door. Sophie left the letter on the table and ran downstairs. Emma and Simon stood on the doorstep. Simon half-smiled. He was nervous.

"Hello," said Emma with determined brightness.

"Come in," said Sophie. Emma walked bravely into the hall. Simon edged his way around the door, staring at the tatty thirteen. Sophie could see he was scared.

"Come up to my room," she said. Emma and Simon followed her upstairs. Sophie closed the door.

"It's not as warm as your house." She shrugged apologetically. "No central heating."

Emma looked around the room, taking in the worn furniture and the faded, threadbare carpet. It seemed a spartan, uncomfortable room. Not like her own which you could walk in with bare feet, your toes sinking into the soft pile of a clean carpet. And cold! Goodness, how cold it was.

"Haven't you got a heater?" Emma asked.

"No. If I want to warm up I go down to the kitchen," Sophie said. "I wear piles of jumpers. I often wear my coat. It's all right. You get used to it."

Emma didn't think she would. She sat down in a huddle on the edge of Sophie's bed and folded her arms. Simon looked out of the window, his face pale. Sophie sensed their discomfort. With nothing to offer but this drab room she became aware of the grime-covered wallpaper, the cracks in the ceiling, the cobweb hanging in the corner, the naked light bulb above her bed.

"I had another experience this morning," she said.

Simon turned abruptly from the window.

"What?"

"I was grabbed from behind when I was standing at the front door."

"Who grabbed you?" Emma asked.

"That's it," said Sophie. "There was no one there." She told about dropping the coal and the bag bursting, about the hissing and the laughter.

"It's weird," said Emma. "Are you sure you didn't imagine it?"

"No," Sophie shook her head. "No, I didn't. The hands really gripped hard but only for a second."

"What did you do?" said Simon.

"I shouted. That's when Mum opened the door and found coal everywhere."

Emma looked about her. Everything around seemed ordinary. Nothing ghostly or terrifying.

"And I saw the face at the window," Sophie said. "Last night."

"You didn't!" gasped Emma. "What was it like?"

"A wispy boy, that's what. Pretty ghostly."

"Wow!" said Emma, impressed. "Have you

34

checked the front door properly for wires yet?" she asked.

"No, not properly, but I can't see any."

"Let's do that now." Emma jumped off the bed. "Come on," she said. Sophie followed. Simon stood staring out of the window, his gaze far away.

Emma ran downstairs and walked purposefully towards the front door. She looked carefully around its edges. She ran her fingers across it.

"Careful!" warned Sophie.

"It's all right," Emma said. She opened it and looked at the tatty thirteen.

"Go on," said Sophie. "Touch it."

Gingerly Emma put her finger on the one. Nothing. She traced her way down it. There was a faint hiss. Emma didn't seem to hear it. She touched the three. Nothing.

"Look!" said Sophie. "Look!"

Emma stood back and stared. Even in the daylight she could see the thirteen brighten and fade. It pulsed bright and faded again.

"Touch it now," said Sophie.

"No fear!"

Sophie moved forward and pressed a finger on to the three. She withdrew it quickly.

"Ouch! Electric shock."

Emma's eyes were wide.

"What's going on?" she said. "There's no wires. It can't be real electricity doing it. So what is?"

"I don't know," said Sophie. "But something is."

Sophie lifted her finger to touch the number again but was distracted by a clatter on the stairs. Simon ran to the front door, his eyes wide and staring. He was going to run straight past them when Emma caught his arm and pinned him to the wall.

"What's the matter?" she demanded.

"I don't know," he panted. "I got scared. I want to go."

"There's nothing to be scared of," said Sophie. "Nothing at all."

At least she didn't think there was. She didn't feel scared. She sensed a danger though. She didn't feel it would harm her but it might harm Simon. His eyes were wild. Slowly a tingling ran up her spine, spreading in fingers across her head. Simon needed to be got away.

"Let's go to Mrs Russett's house," she said. "She's expecting us."

Chapter Five

The children sat in the clutter of Mrs Russett's back room chewing toffee. Gerty was curled up in a bundle on Sophie's lap, her eyes closed but concentrating as Sophie stroked her ears, a loud purr rumbling in her throat.

Chewing toffee had a normality about it that helped Simon to feel more himself. The desire to run and run was a distant memory, the feeling that created the desire a mild discomfort. Something wasn't right but his anxiety about it was fading fast. There was even a little colour in his cheeks.

"Do you like toffee?" asked Mrs Russett, her eyes jumping from one face to another in her eagerness to know. "I make it myself to an old and secret recipe."

"Did you?" said Sophie. "No wonder it's so nice. I've never tasted toffee like it."

"The best in the world," Emma nodded. Her teeth were almost stuck together. She'd helped herself to a large piece. It was taking a lot of chewing.

"Very nice indeed," said Simon. Mrs Russett noticed the distance in his voice. He wasn't quite in the room with them, she thought. She recognized a delicacy in him that neither of the girls had. Both Sophie and Emma had a similar kind of robust strength.

"Another piece anyone?"

There was a chorus of "Yes pleases." Mrs Russett passed the toffee tin round.

"It's nice to have young people in Castle Street," she said as they helped themselves. "That's something I've missed for a while. How do you know Emma, Sophie?"

Sophie hesitated. Emma piped up happily with, "We're in the same class at school."

"I see." Mrs Russett smiled. "And Sophie's a new girl."

"Yes," said Emma.

"And how does that feel, Sophie?"

"Well . . ." Sophie was guarded. She knew Emma was watching her. She felt she had to be careful or she'd give herself away.

"It's all right."

"It takes time to settle in to something new, doesn't it?" said Mrs Russett.

Sophie knew Mrs Russett knew she hated Snareswick School, but did Emma? Emma was in charge and popular, so she was all right. Sophie caught Emma's eye and looked away. Yes, Emma knew. Well, so what?

"Why didn't you tell me number thirteen was a ghost house?" Sophie asked.

Mrs Russett, caught unawares by the question, said, "I thought you knew. You mean, you didn't know?"

"No, of course I didn't. Neither did Mum and Mum still doesn't."

Sophie was aware that she was being accusing and aggressive.

"I see," said Mrs Russett.

"Mum took the house because it was cheap. We haven't got a lot of money. They never said anything about hauntings."

Sophie's anger seemed to spill on to the carpet. It roused Gerty who jumped down and stretched.

"Have you been troubled by anything yet?" Mrs Russett's eyes looked into the distance. "Because a time is coming. I sense a time is coming." Mrs Russett seemed to go far away inside herself. No one said anything. Then she came back again. It was odd.

"What time?" Emma asked.

"Well," Mrs Russet said, "there's a gap between us and them with what you might call a door. The way through. The door is at number thirteen. It wouldn't matter if the house were there or not – the entrance is. In the 1850s when this street was built, number thirteen got built across the gap. It's been causing trouble ever since. The entrance goes way back, you see."

"Who are they? I've seen a creepy face," said Sophie. "And the front door number goes electric without wires."

"I suppose you might call them ghosts," said Mrs Russett. "Or shadows from another time. They will keep dabbling with us."

"How do you know all this?" asked Emma, suddenly suspicious.

"It would be much better if they didn't, of course," said Mrs Russett, not seeming to hear Emma's question. Her eyes went watery.

39

"Once there was a castle. When the street was built in the watercress meadows someone must have remembered as they trampled the green cress to mud."

"To call it Castle Street?" said Sophie.

"But the castle long since vanished. Not a bump in the earth, not a stone of it left. Strange, don't you think? It must have lingered in the air, a shimmering memory. Someone plucked it. It became a thought. 'Castle Street,' they said. 'That's what we'll call it,' as they built the houses and fashioned the pavement. 'Castle Street'."

"There's no record of any castles near here," said Emma. "We did castles at school. How do you know it existed if there are no records. Castle Street's a common enough name."

"How do you think I know?" Mrs Russett's eyes narrowed. It was as if the curls on her head crackled and Sophie saw sparks shoot from them. Esmeralda jumped from her cushion and arched her back. A tingling ran up Sophie's spine almost reassuringly.

Yes, thought Sophie. Mrs Russett is a part of all this.

Mrs Russett repeated her question. Emma pushed her lower lip forward. Her eyes took on a look that said "Don't push me too far, Mrs."

"You're a witch," said Simon. His voice clear, sure, bell-like. "A good witch. You're ever so old, aren't you?"

Emma looked at him as though he'd gone mad. She was beginning to feel distinctly uncomfortable. Ghost, gaps, the normal things of life were getting lost. It made her feel unsure, unsafe and funny inside.

Mrs Russett looked at Simon. He smiled at her.

"The nicest witch in the world," he said.

Emma thought she ought to get Simon away. He looked kind of fragile. All this talk of witches was ridiculous.

"It's been too much for him," she thought. She wanted to stand up, put on her coat and go. But somehow she didn't feel she could. It was nothing to do with being polite or anything like that – she felt incapable of doing it.

"Are you really a witch?" Sophie asked. "Really and truly?"

Emma couldn't believe it. They were both at it. Maybe it was the heat of the room. It *was* hot. Emma could feel her cheeks burn red. Heat filled her head and ran down her nose.

I must look like a beetroot, she thought.

"What's a witch to you?" said Mrs Russett. "I have my powers."

There were sparks. Sophie saw them. Little darts of flashing white light. She saw them and she wasn't afraid. Neither was Simon. Had he seen them? She looked at Emma. Beads of sweat were pouring down her face. It was livid red. She looked feverish. Sophie crossed to her and took Emma's hand in hers.

"It's all right," she said. "We're quite safe."

"It's rubbish!" said Emma, wrenching her hand free. "A load of rubbish! I've never heard anything so utterly stupid in all my life."

"If you resist the knowledge," said Mrs Russett, "you'll make it painful for yourself."

A flash like lightning seared through Emma's head. She felt a pain between her eyes. Her head hurt.

"What are you doing?" she asked.

"Nothing," said Mrs Russett.

Sophie noticed the change in Mrs Russett's voice. It sounded stronger, younger, smooth. She looked at

41

her. Red hair instead of grey sparkled for a moment and was gone.

"Accept the knowledge. Just accept it."

"I'm not going to accept anything!" shouted Emma. "It's ridiculous and *pagan*!" She flung the word insultingly at Mrs Russett, picked up her coat and ran from the room. They heard the front door slam. No one moved.

"Shall we have a cup of tea?" said Mrs Russett. "Or how about a nice hot toddy? She'll come back in a minute."

Simon didn't think so. He wondered if he should go too. He felt a certain disloyalty for staying but felt safe and cocooned, happy at the thought of hot toddy and perhaps another piece of toffee. It was Sophie who got up.

"I think I'll go and find her," she said.

"Yes, that would be nice," said Mrs Russett. "Bring her back for some toddy."

Sophie found Emma at the end of the street. She was kicking a garden wall with her foot and frowning. For a moment Sophie felt she was looking at herself. She recognized in Emma's frown a kind of frustration. Affection and concern welled up inside Sophie. It was going to be difficult for Emma to accept that Mrs Russett had powers, that there was a gap between worlds or realities or whatever you wanted to call it. She, Sophie, had seen the signs and felt the tingling. It was easy for her to accept it.

Emma didn't look up when Sophie stood near her but she stopped kicking. Her coat hung limp and open.

"I just can't believe in that sort of thing," Emma

said. Sophie could see tears in her eyes. She wanted to put her arms round Emma but knew that would be wrong.

"Mrs Russett's making us hot toddy," she said. "You coming?"

"Yeah, in a minute." Sophie left Emma on the pavement and went back indoors.

The toddy was delicious. Something like hot black-currant but not quite. It was spicy and aromatic. Emma smelt it as soon as she pushed open the front door. It reminded her of Christmas. She went sheepishly into the back room. Sophie and Simon already had their hands wrapped around mugs from which they were sipping the fragrant liquid. Mrs Russett handed her a mugful too.

"There you are, Emma. Watch out. It's hot."

"I'm sorry," said Emma. "I didn't mean to be an idiot."

"I'm glad you came back," said Mrs Russett.

Emma sipped her toddy gratefully. She felt welcomed in spite of her struggle not to believe what seemed obvious to everyone else. She remembered she'd seen the thirteen glow and reminded herself to keep an open mind. What did it matter if Mrs Russett called herself a witch? Except that Mrs Russett didn't. It was Simon who had said it. A good witch. Well, she was good and kind, that was obvious.

"The thing is," said Emma, "if this is all true, what do we do?" Mrs Russett put down her mug.

"A good question, Emma. A very good question indeed. What do we do?"

"We thought about forming a ghost-hunting society," said Emma.

Sophie, who had been considering the question carefully, said, "I think we should close the gap. If it stays open Mum is going to be half scared to death. You should have seen her when that face gave her a fright."

"I wonder if scaring us is good fun for them?" said Simon.

"They've been pretty naughty and disruptive over the years," said Mrs Russett. "It makes me think they've enjoyed themselves. They've caused a lot of unnecessary bother."

"People going mad and having to move?" asked Emma.

"That sort of thing," said Mrs Russett. "Now if the gap is closed, make sure they are all on the other side. The last thing we want is one of them stuck with us. Far too much trouble." Simon's eyes widened.

"How are we going to do that?" he said.

There was a knock on the front door. It made Simon jump. Mrs Russett patted him on the arm as she went past.

"We'll manage it somehow," she said.

It was Sophie's mum on the doorstep. She wanted Sophie to know she was on the way to the bus station and she'd left a big plateful of sandwiches on the kitchen table.

"I hope they're not being a nuisance," Mum said.

"Not at all," said Mrs Russett. "They can eat their sandwiches with me if they like."

"I'll go and fetch them," said Sophie. "Bye, Mum."

"Bye, bye, Sophie. Behave yourself, won't you?" said Mum as she set off down the pavement. She turned back.

"Have you got your key?"

44

"It's here," said Sophie, holding it up for her to see. Mum waved and hurried on her way.

Sophie let herself in to the gloom of the hallway. The cold of the house hit her after the warmth of Mrs Russett's back room. She opened the kitchen door and went to the table. The plate of sandwiches was sitting waiting. Gradually Sophie became aware that she was not alone. The tingling began. She watched spellbound as a sandwich lifted itself into the air and disappeared. Another lifted itself and hovered above the plate. Before it could disappear Sophie grabbed it. She put it firmly back with the others, picked up the plate and ran. There was a faint hissing, then silence fell on the empty kitchen.

Chapter Six

When Mrs Russett heard about the sandwich disappearing she warned Sophie to be careful. Sophie
said she would be. It didn't stop her from wanting to
find out where the sandwich had gone. When the
others went home she began looking for it in the
kitchen – on the floor, under the table, in the drawers,
behind the cooker. She couldn't find it.

"How can a sandwich vanish into thin air?" she
wondered.

She looked in the living room, behind the front
door, on the stairs. She went back to the kitchen in
case she'd missed it. It wasn't there.

"Right, I'll try upstairs. Surely a ghost wouldn't
eat it?"

She looked in her room, on the table, under the
bed. She even got a chair and looked on top of the
wardrobe. Apart from a lot of dust there was nothing
there. No, that wasn't right. There *was* something.

"My threepenny bit," she said. It was sitting at the

ack gathering dust. "I didn't put it there. Not unless I've been sleepwalking and I never have before."

Sophie blew the dust from the threepenny bit and put it on her table.

"Amazing!" she said.

She looked in Mum's room. She looked in the bathroom. No sandwich.

"There's still the empty rooms, the attic and Gran's room. I'll try Gran's room next."

Gran's room was small and welcoming. It had the nicest wallpaper of any of the rooms in the house, Sophie thought. The fire was laid out ready in the grate. Gran had only to light it. Sophie looked along the mantlepiece, on the chest of drawers and was about to give up when she noticed something funny about Gran's pillow. There was a bump under the bedspread. Carefully Sophie folded back the bedspread. There was the sandwich sitting on the pillow.

"Ha, ha!" said Sophie. "Very funny."

She picked it up carefully, brushed the crumbs from the pillow and covered the pillow with the bedspread. "I'd have got the blame for that." She was not amused. She looked carefully at the sandwich. It was cheese and cucumber. It seemed all right so she ate it.

She was on her way downstairs, still munching, when the front door opened.

"Sophie, darling!" said Gran. She advanced, her arms outstretched, threatening an embrace. Sophie suffered her cheek to be kissed and her head to be pressed against Gran's bosom. She smelt the pungent, flowery smell of Gran's scent.

"So this is the house. Big, isn't it?" said Gran.

Mum carried Gran's suitcase into the hall and put it down with obvious relief.

"I'll put the kettle on," said Sophie.

"No need," said Gran. "I've brought a tipple. We'll toast the house." She rummaged in her large handbag and pulled out a bottle of sherry.

"Glasses is what we need," she said.

"I'll take your suitcase up," said Sophie. She swallowed the last of her sandwich. "What's for tea, Mum?"

"Give us a chance. Why don't you follow Sophie up, Mum? She can show you your room."

"Lead on," said Gran. She brandished the bottle. Sophie ducked.

Gran seemed to like the room. She opened her suitcase and in no time at all had covered the chest of drawers with an assortment of bottles and bits and bobs. She surveyed her fingers.

"I've scratched my nail varnish. I'll have to do a repair job."

Sophie frowned. She hated the smell of nail varnish. The very thought of it drove her from the room. She went downstairs to see what Mum was doing in the kitchen. The kettle was on. Sophie knew what Mum wanted – a nice cup of tea.

"Have a good day?" Mum asked.

"Yep," said Sophie. "Did you have to wait long?" Mum's face made a grimace.

"Two and a half hours," she said.

"Heavens, Mum!" Sophie was glad she hadn't gone too but she felt sorry for Mum.

"Luckily I had a good book. Snareswick library seems very well stocked. I took out a new book on the way."

"Emma's mum said I can go to their house tomorrow," said Sophie.

"What about your homework?"

"I'll do it tonight. I haven't got much."

By the time Sophie was ready for bed she'd decided she'd had enough of Gran. What with nail varnish smelling out the kitchen and Gran going on and on, asking this, wanting to know that, and would Sophie mind running up to her room for the millionth time to fetch the whatever it was she'd forgotten. It was too much and she was fed up.

"Why can't I have a gran like Mrs Russett who makes toffee and likes cats?" she grumbled. "Instead of one's who's all fluffy and pink and smells of scent."

She looked at her letter to Skinny Tim. It was out of date, she decided. Things were looking up in spite of Gran coming to stay. People were talking to them. Mrs Russett for one and Emma and Simon and Mrs Briggs. She tore the letter up, leaving the pieces on the table.

"I'll write another and tell him all about the hauntings." She yawned. "Tomorrow, maybe." She climbed into bed and snuggled up with her hot-water bottle.

The next morning Sophie noticed that the pieces of Skinny Tim's letter were gone. She put her chair against the wardrobe and climbed up. They weren't there.

"Oh no!" she thought. "Gran's pillow!"

Sure enough, when Gran eventually arrived in the kitchen full of complaints, one of them was she had woken up with bits of torn-up paper all over her. Mum looked at Sophie. Sophie screwed up her face.

"Sorry!" she said. There was no point in scaring

Mum. Better pretend she did it. "Just a joke."

"I don't find that sort of thing funny," said Gran. She brushed a chair with her hand and sat down. "Not funny at all. And all that hissing and giggling woke me up."

"Can I go now, please, Mum?"

"Where's she going?" Gran demanded.

"To visit some friends. Yes, you can go."

Sophie shot from the kitchen as fast as she could before Gran found something else for her to do.

"She has no manners," she heard Gran say as she closed the door. "Didn't even say goodbye."

The three of them sat in Emma's room. Sun streamed in through the window. Sophie thought how ordinary and comfortable it was. It was also warm.

"I don't think *I* could've eaten it," said Simon, his mind on the disappearing sandwich. "I mean, where had it been?" Sophie shrugged.

"It looked all right." She grinned. "And I'm still here."

"Yes," said Simon. Nothing could have persuaded him to eat it, however hungry he was.

"Interesting about the threepenny bit," said Emma. "It's like the whatever it is wants to play practical jokes."

"Yes," said Sophie. "It's not doing anything horrid, is it?"

"Shall we have a ghost hunt?" said Emma. "Mrs Russett didn't say we shouldn't, did she?"

Even Simon agreed they should. He was beginning to feel more at ease about the extraordinary happenings. He felt he was getting used to them.

"I shall want my sword," he said.

Sophie's eyes ran along Emma's bookshelf. She'd never known anyone with so many books before. At the end of the top shelf was a tube. It had *Sneezing Powder* written on the side.

"Does this work?" said Sophie. She picked up the tube for Emma to see.

"I haven't tried it," said Emma. "I had it for my birthday."

Sophie took off the lid. She sniffed at the powder. There was an instant tickling in her nose and she sneezed convulsively three times.

"It works," she said. She rubbed her nose with the back of her hand. "Can I have this for the ghosts?"

"Yes," said Emma. "You're welcome."

"What are you going to take, Em?" Simon asked.

"My canvas groundsheet and some rope," said Emma. "You never know, we might be able to net one."

Sophie wondered about that. Ghosts that could make sandwiches disappear might melt away under groundsheets. But she didn't want to put a damper on things so she didn't say anything.

They arrived at Sophie's house, each clutching the weapon of their choice. As Sophie unlocked the front door and let them in her brow wrinkled into a frown.

"Don't forget my gran's here," she said.

Sophie peeped into the kitchen. Mum had fallen asleep over her library book. There was no sign of Gran. She closed the door quietly and went back to the others.

"Let's start at the top of the house and work down," she said.

Emma ran her hands over the back of the front door.

"Anything there?" said Simon. Emma shook her head.

"They come and they go, it seems," said Sophie. "Let's go up to the attic."

To get into the attic, which was Sophie's favourite hiding place, you had to go to the top of the house and into the end room. The attic was reached by a door halfway up the wall. There was a chair already underneath the door, left from Sophie's last visit.

Sophie opened the attic door and climbed on to the chair. Simon drew his sword. Emma's knuckles tightened around the rope. Sophie went first. It took a few moments for her eyes to get used to the half-light.

"Come on up," she said. "I don't think there's anything up here."

The others clambered up behind her. No, it didn't feel in the least bit ghostly.

"It's nice, isn't it?" said Sophie. "I come up here sometimes to be on my own. I sit here." She pointed to a small stool under the dirt-stained skylight. "You can just about read a book."

"It's a bit dirty," said Emma. She noticed long and complicated cobwebs woven amongst the rafters. "What do spiders feed on up here?"

Simon sheathed his sword. He could see it would be a good place for a den. It seemed warmer than the rest of the house.

"It's nice," he said. "Very nice."

They were beginning to relax when there was a terrific bang.

"Quick!" said Sophie. "Someone's shut the door!" She pushed it. "And they've locked it, the stinking

52

beasts! Help me push, you two!"

They pushed. The door wouldn't budge. They tried harder. It was no use. It wasn't going to open.

"That's odd," said Sophie. "The door's only fastened with a wooden peg. We've pushed hard enough to break the peg but the door hasn't moved the tiniest bit."

"How are we going to get out?" said Simon, a note of rising panic in his voice. Emma put an arm around his shoulder.

"Don't worry! If the worst comes to the worst we can shout or even break the skylight and climb on to the roof," she said.

The tingling began in Sophie's spine.

"Ha, ha!" she said. "Ha, ha! Very clever. Yah boo sucks to you!" She stuck her tongue out, pulled the worst face she could manage and kicked the door. It swayed gently open.

"Typical!" said Sophie. "Come on, you two."

"What was all that about?" said Emma.

"I don't know," said Sophie. "But it seemed to work." She jumped out of the attic and ran to the landing. Nothing and no one was to be seen.

"But the door was locked," said Emma. "We all pushed."

"Not locked," said Sophie. "Held."

"You okay, Simon?" said Emma. Simon nodded. He was shaken.

"Let's get after them or it or whatever it was," said Sophie. They looked in all the other rooms except Gran's.

"Probably having a nap." Sophie raised her eyebrows and pulled a face. "The last thing we want to do is wake her."

By the time they reached downstairs they were

beginning to feel the whatever it was had eluded them.

"Ah!" said Sophie. "One place we haven't looked is the cellar." She opened the door at the back of the stairs.

"That's funny," she said in a low voice. "The light's on."

Rustling noises drifted up to them. Simon drew his sword.

"Stand by with the groundsheet," whispered Sophie. She pulled the top off the sneezing powder tube. She beckoned them to follow her. More rustling was heard, followed by something clinking.

"Ready?" mouthed Sophie. Emma nodded.

As they turned the corner on the stairs, Sophie shot sneezing powder into the air and Emma, with amazing sleight of hand, sent the groundsheet billowing over the whatever it was. There was a wail of dismay followed by paroxysms of sneezing. The groundsheet thrashed and billowed. Eventually it fell to the floor revealing Gran, her hair wild, her eyes running as she sneezed and sneezed.

"What do you mean by this?" she raged through her sneezing. Sophie could see she was furious. Her neat hair was tousled and her nail varnish was bound to be scratched.

"Sorry, Gran. Sorry. We thought you were a . . . Sorry."

"I'll give you sorry!" she yelled. "You're an ill-mannered brat. And more brats. Who are they?"

"This is Emma and this is Simon. We didn't know you were down here. Honest."

Gran looked mean in her fury. Sophie wished she was anywhere but where she was. The sudden tingling surprised her. It ran up her spine and across

54

her scalp, pressing into her forehead. The children stared. Slowly, without Gran seeming to notice, the hair on her head began to rise. Soon it stuck straight out in all directions. Simon's eyes widened. Emma gaped. Sophie grinned, in spite of herself. Gran saw the grin and became dangerous. The sound of footsteps on the stairs behind them and Mum's voice asking, "What on earth's going on down there?" came just in time to stop Gran from taking a swipe at Sophie.

In an instant Gran's hair fell back on her head and the tingling stopped. All that was left was for Sophie to face the music.

"But", thought Sophie, "it was worth it to see Gran looking like that."

"I think it's time Emma and Simon went home," said Mum. "When you've said goodbye, Sophie, you're to come straight to the kitchen." Mum took Gran by the arm and helped her up the cellar steps leaving the children, somewhat subdued, to follow on behind.

Chapter Seven

Emma was already at the bus stop when Sophie and Mum arrived on Monday morning. Emma noticed Sophie's frown. She said hello and left it at that. Sophie managed a sort of grunt. Her mum looked worn out.

When Sophie's mum got off Emma said. "What about the hair? I've never seen anything like it. It stood on end. Really stood on end."

"Yeah," said Sophie. She looked depressed. "That was the worst Sunday evening of my life. Gran's got me marked down as a delinquent. Great, isn't it?"

"I think we should have a ghost-hunter's meeting tonight," said Emma.

"We'll have to have it at your house," said Sophie. "I've been confined to my room for the rest of the week."

"But it's an ice-box!" said Emma. "That's cruelty to children."

"Do you know what she was doing? Looking to see

if there was any wine in the cellar. That's typical of my gran."

Sophie didn't mind about being confined to her room. She could always get into bed to warm up. There was even a bonus – no Gran to put up with all evening.

"It's going to be tricky getting out," she said.

The bus came to a jolting stop. Pupils for Snareswick School tumbled noisily on to the pavement. Sophie hardly noticed the scramble.

"I think I'll climb down the plane tree," she decided as she and Emma were jostled along.

"Stop shoving!" Emma snapped at a freckle-nosed boy swinging his school bag. The boy slouched off and space appeared around them. Emma regained her composure and returned her attention to Sophie.

"You mean get on to it from your bedroom window?" she asked.

"Why not? If I can get the bedroom window open it should be easy." Emma looked doubtful.

"If you fell you could break a leg or even worse."

"I won't," said Sophie. "The only problem will be the window. I've never tried opening it. It may be stuck."

Emma was doubtful but kept her thoughts to herself.

"I'll be round at half past seven," Sophie said.

They turned into the school gates. Emma linked her arm into Sophie's as they walked towards the school building.

"Okay," she said.

Sophie felt a glow of pleasure and pride well up inside her. She had a friend. It felt good.

The school day passed in a kind of haze for Sophie, her mind only half on her lessons. Emma's obvious choice of her as a companion had placed her high in the esteem of her classmates, but she was too preoccupied to notice. Her frown was in evidence but it was a frown of concentration, not aggression.

By the end of the day Sophie had planned her exit from the window and descent down the tree in detail. The problem, she knew, would be getting back up again. She must remember to take her key in case she couldn't manage it. If the worst came to the worst she could try sneaking in the front door. With luck no one would notice.

At the end of the day Emma and Sophie stood on the pavement outside Sophie's house. They looked up at the plane tree.

"Are you sure you can do it?" said Emma.

"I've worked it all out," said Sophie. "I need some rope, that's all. There's a piece in the attic that should do."

"If you're going to the attic for heaven's sake don't get locked in," said Emma.

"I won't." Sophie grinned and put her key in the door. "Bye!" she said.

"Bye!" said Emma. "See you later, then."

Gran was in the kitchen working out her football pools.

"Hello, Gran. I'm back."

"So I see," said Gran. She hardly bothered to look up. Sophie could see she wasn't forgiven. She closed the door and went up to her room. She changed into her oldest pair of jeans and her favourite green sweater with the hole in it. She noticed her threepenny bit was gone from her table and fetched it from the top of the wardrobe.

"I wonder why the whatever it is keeps putting it up there?" she thought as she jumped down from her chair. This time she didn't leave the threepenny bit on the table. She put it in her pocket.

Next, she went up to the attic. When her eyes had accustomed themselves to the half light she dragged out the piece of rope. She shook off the dust and coiled it neatly round her arm. She stood quietly for a moment and listened. Nothing. She shut the attic door and took the rope to her room. It seemed strong enough.

Sophie moved her table away from the window, positioning it under the light bulb.

"Better for doing homework, anyway," she said.

She undid the window catch and pushed. For a moment she didn't think the window was going to budge. Then it rattled upwards, the sash weights clanking noisily. She looked outside and smelt the damp evening air. The branch that tapped her window tickled her face. The end nearest the tree might just be strong enough to take her weight if she jumped for it. If she missed, with luck she would land on the privet hedge below. A nice cushion for a fall. Once she had tied the rope to the tree she'd be able to come and go as she pleased. She could loop the rope around the branch after she'd climbed up, ready to drop down again when needed. She hoped no one would notice it hanging while she was at Emma and Simon's. She would hide the end in the privet hedge.

Sophie was distracted by hurrying footsteps coming down the pavement. It was Mum carrying a heavy bag of shopping. She pulled her window shut and wondered whether to go downstairs and offer to help. The front door banged. No, Gran would only point out how awful she was. If they had been on their own she and Mum would have made up long ago. She decided to stay where she was. That way Gran wouldn't have any reason for complaint. She began her homework.

At half past six there was a knock on her door. It was Mum. She came in and sat on the bed. She sighed.

"You were right, Sophie," she said at last. "It would have been better if Gran hadn't come. It's all too much."

Sophie sat next to her and put her arms round Mum's shoulders.

"I'm sorry," she said. "I didn't mean to upset her."

"Whatever were you doing?" said Mum. "You must've known she was down there."

Sophie was torn between telling the truth and making up something so Mum wouldn't be scared. She decided on the truth. With luck Mum wouldn't take it seriously. She seemed to have forgotten about the horrid face at the window.

"We were ghost-hunting."

"Ghost-hunting!" Mum burst out laughing. "And you mean you thought Gran was a ghost?" Sophie nodded. "Good gracious! Well, you certainly caught your ghost."

"Not quite," thought Sophie and grinned at the memory of Gran in a rage with her hair standing on end.

"You coming down for something to eat?" asked Mum. Sophie shook her head.

"Do you mind if I don't?"

"No," said Mum. "I'll bring your tea up for you."

★   ★   ★

When Sophie had finished eating she put the tray on the landing and pinned a notice to her door which said, "Please Do Not Disturb". She looked at her watch. Seven-fifteen.

"Better get going," she thought. She switched off the light and drew back the curtains. Try as she might the window rattled horribly when she opened it. Fortunately, the kitchen was at the back of the house but a man walking along the pavement looked about him, trying to locate the sound. Sophie ducked back into the room until he was gone. She checked the street. It was deserted.

She slipped her head through the coil of rope and pulled it over her shoulder. She climbed on to the windowsill and gauged her jump. It was difficult to see in the dark. She was concentrating so hard she didn't hear the hissing or see behind her, just visible in the light from the window, the shadow of a huge arched door gliding across the carpet.

Sophie jumped. It was a well-judged leap. She should have made the branch easily but instead of reaching the tree in a slight downward arc she was propelled upward. The force beneath her took her unawares. She gasped. But it was as though part of her expected it. The force left her breathless, clinging to the top of the tree.

Sophie stayed there a moment or two, recovering from her surprise. She looked down and saw the curtains pulled violently into her room. There was no wind outside. It was suction from a mighty draught from within. She was fascinated.

"What next?" she wondered. There was nothing. The curtains fell back and became still. Sophie began to climb down the tree. She did so carefully. She reached the branch she had originally aimed for and

61

balancing on it, tied the rope securely to the branch above and let it drop.

It was only then that Sophie allowed herself to look into her room. It was an astonishing sight. Everything was in chaos. Her school books were strewn everywhere, the table upturned, the mattress from her bed leaned lopsidedly against the wall. The wave of energy had left destruction.

"I just hope Mum doesn't go in," she thought. She crossed her fingers. "She'll think I've flipped if she does."

Hand over hand and balancing herself against the tree with her feet she lowered herself to the ground. She tucked the rope into the privet hedge. Then she ran before anyone could stop her. Her footsteps pounded along the pavement. If she had turned she would have seen the curtains at her window billow into the street as something powerful and invisible arched its way on to the pavement, stirring leaves as it went, leaving a trail of Sophie's school papers fluttering in the gutter.

It wasn't until she had knocked at the Briggs' front door that Sophie heard the hissing behind her. She turned, her heart beating with loud thumps. She stood transfixed as a towering shape rose from a swirl of powdery white wisps. It was cloaked in white, a hood across its face. Sophie took a step towards it as if pulled forward. The door opened behind her, silhouetting Emma in light. Emma gasped, took in the scene in an instant, darted forward and, with great presence of mind, pulled Sophie into the safety of the house and slammed the door.

They both leaned against the hall wall. Sophie

drooped on trembling legs. She let out a gasp and slid down the wall until she was sitting on the floor. For the moment they were both too shocked to speak.

"Phew!" said Sophie at last. "What was that?" Then, regaining her nerve, "Quick! Upstairs."

She ran up the stairs two at a time and dashed into Emma's room. She switched off the light and pulled back the curtains. The street was deserted. There was nothing there. Emma followed her up and hung back by the door.

"It's all right," said Sophie. "It's gone."

"Are you sure?"

"Yes, it's not there."

"I feel sick," said Emma, sitting on her bed.

"Shock," said Sophie. "I don't think we should tell Simon. Where is he by the way?"

"Watching TV."

"I think we should tell Mrs Russett."

"When?"

"Now," said Sophie.

Chapter Eight

It took all Emma's courage to venture out into the
street. There was a tightness in her stomach which
spread through her whole body. It made her tense
and ready for flight. Sophie seemed much more
relaxed, excited even. She began to run along the
pavement. Emma followed with more caution. She
was reluctant to risk another frightening encounter.

There was a chill in the air. The damp smell of wet
leaves teased Emma's nostrils. It seemed so ordinary
walking down the street. This October night was just
like any other. A friendly darkness. That's how she'd
always felt before as the darkness of winter had
begun. She mustn't fool herself. This was different,
unreal even. Not in her wildest imaginings had she
dreamed she would see anything like the figure on the
pavement. Something so terrifying outside her own
front door! But she had seen it. There was no denying
it. Ghosts *did* exist.

They passed Sophie's house on the other side of

the street. Sophie's room was in darkness with the window open as she had left it. There was no sense of disturbance. All was still.

"Oh, no!" cried Sophie. Before Emma could stop her she had crossed the street. She began to collect the scattered bits of school work which had spilled from her window in turmoil and lay strewn untidily along the pavement and in the gutter.

"That's too bad." Sophie was cross. "What a mess. What a rotten mess."

Summoning up her courage Emma crossed the street. Keeping a wary eye open she bent to help.

"It'll all have to be written out again," Sophie moaned. "It's my essay and it's filthy."

"I'll give you a hand if you like," Emma said.

"Would you?" said Sophie. Then her face fell. "No good," she said. "They'll know I didn't write it by the handwriting. They'll think someone else did my homework."

"We could explain," said Emma.

"Don't be daft. Who'd believe us?" Emma shrugged.

"No one." She wouldn't believe such a story if it wasn't happening to her. She only believed it because it was.

Clutching the soggy papers they hurried to Mrs Russett's house and knocked on the front door. A car drove down Castle Street as they were waiting. It was somehow reassuring. Emma relaxed a little. Sophie was still excited. After what seemed like an age a light came on in the hall. It shone from the gap under the door. There was a shuffling and unlocking.

"Who is it?" said a voice. Sophie didn't recognize it as Mrs Russett's.

"It's Emma and me, Sophie," she said.

The door opened. The figure in the doorway, lit from behind by the hall light, seemed too tall to be Mrs Russett.

"Come in."

But it was Mrs Russett. She closed the door. They stood waiting, both aware of a difference, not sure what it was. Mrs Russett fastened the door and they followed her along the hallway. They were met by the cosy clutter of the back room and Mr Spiv's obvious pleasure at seeing them. He curled himself around their ankles, brushing his tail affectionately against their legs. Gerty, from her place on the table, stretched languidly and yawned. Esmeralda opened an eye and watched.

"You have something to tell me and I have something to tell you," said Mrs Russett. The strength of Mrs Russett's voice drew Sophie's attention from Mr Spiv's ears to her face. Emma was already staring.

"The door is open," said Mrs Russett. "Open wide. Someone of power is on our side. I am ready and am waiting."

There was a pulsing energy in the room. Sophie could feel it. Mrs Russett's hair stood from her head, red and alive. Emma took a step back until she felt a chair press into her knees, forcing her to sit. Fear crept in through her toes until it filled her whole body. It left her powerless and frozen, facing the unknown.

Sophie knew the energy flowed from Mrs Russett. It hit her as the tingling ran up her spine. Mrs Russett looked past her to the door. Sophie's eyes followed. Mrs Russett's gaze was fixed on something coming under the door. Tentacles of powdery white mist were invading the room. Mr Spiv arched his back.

66

His eyes glinted. He jumped on to the table and stood his ground. Gerty took several quick leaps until she was beside Esmeralda. Then she too turned, arched wild and ready. Esmeralda let out a long, threatening growl.

Slowly, as before, the wisps grew, arranging and rearranging their long fingers into the towering form. It seemed it would go on forever but it must only have been for a few seconds. The hooded figure stood before them, sinister and silent. The hissing began. The figure lifted its arms and took the hood from its head. Sophie was spellbound. The face had the same gaunt, hollow eyes as the face at the window. It stared with a grave intensity at Mrs Russett. The hissing grew stronger. A wind blew across the room, lifting Mrs Russett's hair from her face.

"The key!" it said. The figure lifted an arm towards Mrs Russett as if expecting her to give it.

"I do not have it," came Mrs Russett's reply. Her eyes shone orange like glowing coals. "It is lost."

"It must be found," said the figure. "The door must be closed. Forever."

Mrs Russett nodded her head slowly.

"We are agreed," she said. "The door must be closed."

"The key is here," said the figure. It gestured sweepingly around the room. Yet Sophie knew it didn't mean in the room but on this side of the door. "It must be found or we suffer the consequences."

The hissing was shrill as the figure turned. Things scattered across the room. Sophie felt her hair blow across her face and herself pulled towards the figure as the wind sucked at her.

"Resist it, Sophie," commanded Mrs Russett. "You do not need to go beyond the door."

Then the figure was gone. Straight through Mrs Russett's living room wall as if it were not there. Esmeralda stopped growling but her eyes stayed wide. Her coat was ruffled and she didn't like it. Gerty jumped on to Mrs Russett's shoulders and Mr Spiv protested with a long, loud miaow.

"It's all over, puss cats," said Mrs Russett. "For the moment."

Emma, who had sat rigid throughout the figure's visit, let out a sob and then another. Sophie put her arm around her friend's shoulder.

"It's gone now," she said.

"I don't believe in ghosts," Emma said. "I don't. I don't."

"There, there, Emma," said Mrs Russett, her old self. With gentle fingertips she stroked Emma's hair. "That's the trouble with these things. It's a bit of a shock. But it won't hurt you. There, there, love."

"Did it really walk through the wall?" said Emma.

"The wall, the door, they mean no more to it than running your hand through a puff of smoke. That's how it is. Don't trouble yourself, love," said Mrs Russett soothingly.

Emma tried to put the disorderly things that were happening into an order in her head.

"It's mind-boggling, that's all," she said.

"It is and it isn't," said Sophie. To her it was perfectly understandable and acceptable. She wondered why. It seemed almost ordinary. She caught Mrs Russett smiling at her and smiled back.

"Toffee, anyone?" said Mrs Russett.

"Yes, please," said Sophie.

Chewing toffee helped Emma to feel a little better. It

68

comforted her shattered nerves and distracted her as she picked stuck toffee from a tooth with her finger.

"Who was it?" said Sophie. "The man in the robes?"

"I'm not sure, dear," said Mrs Russett. "We've not met before. I can't think what all that effort was about. It takes a lot, you know, for them to materialize on our side."

"Where is the door? That's what I want to know," said Sophie. "I wouldn't mind going through it."

"Sophie, you mustn't," said Emma, anxiety contorting her face. "Please, don't."

"Well, I can't anyway," said Sophie, "because I don't know where it is."

Esmeralda let out a low growl. Mrs Russett turned as something caught her eye.

"Oh!" she said. "We have another visitor." Emma saw nothing. Mrs Russett was following an invisible thing around the room with her eyes.

"What are you looking at?" asked Sophie.

"Can't you see him, Sophie?" Mrs Russett seemed surprised. "Look carefully."

The tingling began again. Sophie looked. She became aware of a wispy grey shadow. Yet it wasn't a shadow. It couldn't have been. It was under the electric light. The shadow came uncertainly towards her.

"What does it want?"

"What have you got?" said Mrs Russett.

"Nothing."

"You have. There's something in your pocket he wants." Sophie remembered the threepenny bit.

"It's this," she said, and laid it on the palm of her hand. The shadow bounded towards her. It lifted the threepenny bit from her hand. Emma gasped when

69

she saw the threepenny bit floating in the air. Then it was gone and the shadow with it.

"Just like the sandwich," said Sophie as the tingling stopped. "I bet it ends up on top of the wardrobe again."

"Likes threepenny bits, does he?" said Mrs Russett with a smile. "Well, he should be on the other side of the door. He's out to make mischief, the little imp."

"Was it him who did Gran's hair, do you think?" Sophie laughed. "I bet it was."

Mrs Russett didn't answer. She absent-mindedly handed round the toffee tin. She was thinking hard. She knew it was important to find the key to the door. The energy began again. Mrs Russett stood up. She seemed to grow and her hair became wild with tiny lights.

"It is for you to find the key, Sophie. You have the gift," she said.

Mrs Russett's eyes flashed fire and Sophie found herself falling into blackness, the taste of toffee overwhelming her until she saw she was in a tunnel at the end of which was a large studded door. She knew that beyond the door was a dungeon. It was chilling and damp. Let into the stonework, quite high up on the wall, was a ledge. On the ledge she could see an iron key. She reached upwards. As she did so she found herself standing in front of Mrs Russett, who stood no longer tall but tired and old. The vibrant energy had gone from her. Gently Sophie took her arm and led her to a chair. Mrs Russett sank thankfully into it.

"Did you see it?" she asked. Her voice was weak.

"I did," said Sophie.

"See what?" asked Emma, not understanding.

"The key," said Sophie.

"You must find it, Sophie," said Mrs Russett softly. "I know you will. Then everything will be laid to rest." Her eyes began to droop. "It's time for you to go home. Be careful going up that tree," she said.

Sophie and Emma tiptoed from the room. Mrs Russett nodded asleep with Gerty curled contentedly on her lap. Mr Spiv sat on the arm of her chair washing his paws. They closed the front door quietly behind them. Once on the pavement Sophie folded up the bits of paper that were to have been her homework and stuffed them into her back pocket. When they got to number thirteen the house was quiet. Emma glanced at the tatty numbers on the door. They didn't glow. There was no hissing.

"That's it for tonight," said Sophie. She pulled the rope from the privet hedge. "I'd better go and clear up the mess," she added.

"Be careful," said Emma. "What shall I tell Simon?"

"Everything," said Sophie. "It's all right."

With those words she swung from the rope and began to climb. Emma watched her. Sophie hauled up the rope and jumped safely to the windowsill. She waved. Emma returned the wave and ran for home as fast as her legs would take her.

Chapter Nine

Sophie closed the window as quietly as she could and turned to survey the mess. Even in the street light she could see it would take a while to clear up. She drew the curtains and felt her way to the light switch, pausing to listen to the sounds in the rest of the house. Distant music was coming from the kitchen. Mum and Gran had the radio on.

"It's amazing they didn't hear the furniture when it swirled about," she thought. She switched on the light and let out a groan. "It's not funny," she said. "Not funny at all."

The only piece of furniture which was still in place was the wardrobe, but its doors had swung open and the contents were scattered everywhere.

"Just as well the wardrobe didn't move," grumbled Sophie as she collected the clothes. "I'd never have got it back against the wall. Much too heavy."

Clearing up took ages. At last her clothes were put

away, the table was standing upright, her mattress was back on the bed and the bed made. Sophie sat beside the jumble of papers she had collected on the table. She pulled the crumpled remnants of the essay from her pocket and sighed.

"I'll be up all night doing this. It's not fair." She pulled at a lock of ginger hair and curled it round her finger. As she gazed at the mess of papers in despair a shadow flickered near the wardrobe. Sophie felt her eyelids grow heavy. Fatigue began to creep over her. Any will to begin writing seeped out of her. Her only thought was for a nice hot-water bottle to cuddle as she snuggled up in bed.

"I'll get up early and sort it out before breakfast," she told herself. "I must. I've got to hand it in tomorrow." She picked up her hot-water bottle and opened her bedroom door.

"I suppose I'll have to talk to Gran." She listened. The music was still playing. Leaving her door open she tiptoed downstairs. The flickering shadow moved from the wardrobe across the room. Sophie's bedroom door began to close. By the time she reached the bottom of the stairs it had shut with a gentle click.

Sophie went into the kitchen and surveyed the scene. Mum was asleep, her head resting on her chest, a newspaper on her lap. Gran was leaning over the table. Some large fluffy pink garment on knitting needles lay by her but Gran wasn't knitting. She was putting the finishing touches to her nail varnish.

Before she could help herself Sophie's nose had wrinkled and she had said, "Pooh!"

"That's enough from you, young lady!" Gran snapped. Her lips pursed. "Isn't it time you were in bed? It's half-past ten."

73

"I've come to fill my hot-water bottle," said Sophie.

She moved quickly round the table, brushing Mum on her way to the cooker. Mum woke with a start.

"Now look what you've done, clumsy child!" Gran spat the words at her.

"Sorry, Mum," said Sophie.

"Fill the kettle right up, Sophie," said Mum with a yawn. "I think it's time we all went to bed. Have you finished your homework?"

"Yes, sort of."

"What kind of reply is that," said Gran. "You either have finished or you haven't."

Sophie bit her lip. She turned to the sink and ran water into the kettle.

Horrid old bat, she thought. Why does she have to be so mean? I've never done anything to her. Not on purpose. Sophie let out a big sigh. She plonked the kettle on to the stove and looked for the matches.

"Can't you ever do anything in a ladylike manner?" snapped Gran. "My nerves won't take much more of this. Crash, bang, wallop!"

"Don't, Mum. Sophie's tired, that's all."

"You go right on and defend her. You usually do. Perhaps you could bring my hot-water bottles up. I'm going to bed."

Gran swept up her knitting and nail varnish and departed upstairs. Mum quietly closed the kitchen door behind her. Sophie slumped down on the table and put her head in her hands.

"The kettle's going to take ages to heat up. How many bottles does she want?"

"Two," said Mum, turning off the radio. "What's up?"

Mum ran her hand over Sophie's curls. Sophie turned and buried her face in Mum's cardigan.

"I didn't mean to upset her. I really didn't. It was all a mistake. And then what with the hair standing up, I couldn't help laughing."

Sophie froze. She hadn't meant to mention the hair. Mum stroked Sophie's curls over and over. She watched them spring and bounce, spring and bounce as if mesmerized. She hadn't taken in what Sophie had said about the hair. She was deep in her own thoughts.

"It's chemistry, I suppose," said Mum. "If you don't get on I suppose you don't and that's that. No reason why you should really."

"You only get on because you do everything she says."

"Sophie!"

"Well, you do."

The lid on the kettle rattled. Mum took Sophie's hot-water bottle from the table and began to fill it. She screwed in the stopper and shook out the drips.

"Here, go on. Take it and scram." She gave Sophie a quick kiss. "See you in the morning and sleep tight, love."

"Night, night, Mum," Sophie said, clasping the hot-water bottle to her. "I don't suppose I could borrow your alarm clock?"

"Whatever for?"

"I want to get up early."

"No, you can't," said Mum. "I don't want to chance you switching it off and going back to sleep."

"That's what I thought you'd say," said Sophie. "Night!"

"Goodnight," said Mum. She watched her daughter go and smiled a faint, tired smile before turning to fill the other hot-water bottles.

Sophie opened her bedroom door and closed it behind her. She shivered as the cold of her room closed in on her. She pulled back the bedspread, wrapped her nightdress around the hot-water bottle and stuffed it under the bedclothes to warm up. She looked at her essay. Her gasp was echoed by a faint hissing.

"I don't believe it! I don't believe it!"

The papers she had left in a muddled pile had been carefully sorted. The crumpled essay she had retrieved from the road was on top and next to it was a copy written out in a passable imitation of her own handwriting. It was unfinished as though the writer had been disturbed, but most of it was done all the same.

"Thank you!" cried Sophie, looking about her. "Thank you whoever you are."

Tears of gratitude pricked her eyes as she pulled off her clothes and scrambled for her nightie. She jumped hurriedly into bed. She would finish the copying in the morning.

"I wish I knew who'd done it," she whispered as she snuggled up, hot-water bottle held tight. She turned out the light with a sigh and was asleep almost as soon as her head touched the pillow.

The room was still. In the quiet Sophie's regular breathing could be heard coming from the bed. Then, ever so gently, the plane tree branch tap-tapped against the window as if someone was asking to come in. There was a faint hissing and a crack of light appeared across the carpet as if made by some huge and heavy door being pushed ajar. Through the green-yellow crack stepped the shadow figure of a boy, hollow-eyed, pale and slender. The light made a pathway. Along this he stepped, looking first at the bed and the sleeping Sophie and then towards the table. Light from the narrow opening glowed across Sophie's essay, turning the paper a shade of pale green. The boy bent over the paper and, lifting the pen, began to write. Slowly and carefully he finished copying Sophie's essay.

The knock on the door was loud but then it wasn't the first knock. It penetrated Sophie's sleep, forcing her into a wakefulness she didn't want. She groaned. The door opened. Mum's irritated voice said. "I'm not telling you again, Sophie. It's now ten to eight. You've got twenty minutes. Please get up."

Sophie made herself sit up and blinked hard to keep her eyes open.

"Ten to eight?"

"That's what I said. Your breakfast's on the table. I'm not telling you again." The door slammed shut.

Sophie half-fell out of bed. She crossed the room to pull back the curtains, forgetting the table was under the light. Her toe collided with a table leg. She let out a yelp of pain and hopped the rest of the way to the window. She drew back the curtains and studied the toe for signs of blood. There were none and she could move it. She returned to look at her work on the table, trying to think of a plausible excuse for Miss Pennyforth.

"I didn't finish my essay because . . ." She rubbed her eyes. She picked up the essay and let out a yelp of delight.

"It's finished! Somebody's finished it! I could hug

them," she cried. Grabbing her clothes she ran for the warmth of the bathroom. She washed and dressed under the glow of the electric heater. With an amazing feat of memory she turned the heater off, collected her school things, including the precious essay, and ran downstairs to the kitchen.

"I hope you remembered to leave the heater on for your Gran," said Mum as Sophie burst into the kitchen. Sophie groaned, dropped everything and ran back upstairs. Too late. The bathroom door closed in her face. Irritable mutterings could be heard as the heater switch clicked back on. Sophie leaned her head against the door as her face screwed into its famous frown.

"No," she thought. "No, I won't let it get to me. A genuine error. I didn't mean it." She turned and raced back downstairs to eat as much breakfast as she could manage in the time she had left.

Sophie and Mum arrived at the bus stop very out of breath. Sophie was clutching a piece of cold toast which she stuffed into her mouth as the bus arrived. Emma was waiting patiently for news with a suppressed look of excitement on her face. Sophie did nothing but grunt and chew. Mum, disapproving, didn't say anything.

The bus was full. Sophie and Emma stood shoulder to shoulder. Mum had her back to them. Sophie shot Emma a warning glance. It was a don't-talk-to-me frown. Emma took the hint. The bus turned sharply into the High Street and jolted to a stop. Mum said goodbye and got off. Sophie pulled Emma from the lap of a large woman, where she had landed when the bus had swung round the corner.

The woman clearly thought she had done it on purpose.

"I'm sorry," said Emma. "I really am."

The woman brushed her lap and tut-tutted. Emma turned to Sophie and pulled a face. Sophie felt the woman looking at her and stifled a grin.

"What happened?" said Emma. "Did your mum find out?"

"No," said Sophie. "It was amazing. My room looked like a tornado had hit it. It took ages to sort out. But they didn't hear a thing. Mum was asleep when I went down and Gran was listening to the radio. Incredible!"

"What are you going to do about your essay?" Emma asked. "You could say you were ill or something."

"No need."

"You got it done then?" Sophie nodded.

"Yup. But not by me. By the boy." Emma's eyes widened.

"The threepenny bit boy," said Sophie. "It must have been. Who else could've done it?"

"You mean someone else rewrote it? What about your gran?"

"Don't be daft! She thinks I'm the pits."

The bus pulled up sharply at the school bus stop. This time Emma was ready for the jerk. She avoided the woman's lap and swung into Sophie. Sophie gave her a shove.

"Come on. Hurry up. I want to show it to you."

Sophie took out the essay in the cloakroom. She didn't want to draw attention to it as it was a forgery.

"It's really good. Just like your writing," said Emma. "How clever."

"Lucky, more like. I was going to get up early this

morning and rewrite it but I overslept." The bell rang.

"I wish we could get to know this boy, don't you?" said Sophie.

"That's what Simon says," said Emma. "How do we do it?"

"Maybe we could leave him a note?" said Sophie. "If he can write he must be able to read. He might be able to help find the key."

Emma swung round the door of their classroom into the noisy throng.

"It gives me the shudders, all of it," Emma said.

"But I've got to do it. Mrs Russett said I was the one. Remember?" Emma nodded. She had a feeling in her stomach that reminded her of going to the dentist.

"If Sophie's not scared, I'm not going to be," she told herself.

Easier said than done, of course. Emma plunged herself into the school day, leaving Sophie to muse over how she would find the key and the extraordinary things that had happened at home.

Chapter Ten

The next few days were uneventful. Sophie tried to concentrate on her school work but found it difficult. She wanted to think of plans for talking to the boy and finding the key. Her thoughts kept returning to these problems. At home she spent her evenings composing notes to the boy. She left them out last thing at night in her room. She wanted to leave them all over the house but thought it unwise.

"I don't want Gran getting her hands on them. I'd never hear the end of it. And I don't want Mum frightened either," she thought. It was to no avail. Not even the simple note in big capitals, PLEASE GET IN TOUCH, elicited the slightest response.

By Friday evening Mum tried hard to persuade Sophie to come and eat with her and Gran in the kitchen.

"Oh go on, love," Mum said. "All is forgiven."

"No, really Mum. I'd rather not. I seem to do things wrong. Better if I stay up here. Anyway, Emma says can I go round to her house tonight? Can I?" Mum nodded.

"Back by nine o'clock sharp," she said. "I'll bring your tea up."

But it wasn't Mum who brought her tea up – it was Gran. She plonked the tray on the table and looked around the room. Sophie watched her. She was cold and sat huddled on the bed with her coat on.

"I don't know why you stay in this ice-box when we've said you can be downstairs," said Gran. "Trying to get out of the washing-up, I suppose. Laziness is not something I like in young people." Her eyes narrowed. "Or are you up to something else?"

Sophie kept her gaze steady and said, "I don't know what you mean."

"Don't you now?" said Gran. "I wonder."

With that she swished from the room, leaving the lingering smell of her scent.

"What a cheek!" Sophie thought. Her face flushed hot at the unexpected invasion. "What a nerve! What if I *am* up to something? It's nothing to do with her."

She sat at the table and began her food. She was hungry and the meal was already cool but it was good. One of Mum's bean and vegetable casseroles. She would have liked some more but had no intention of asking while Gran was in the kitchen. She noticed the PLEASE GET IN TOUCH note beside her on the table and turned it face down. She collected all the other notes she had written, tore them into tiny pieces and dropped them into the wastepaper basket.

"Just in case she comes nosing when I'm out."

Sophie picked up the tray. Switching off the light

with her chin she went downstairs. Getting the kitchen door open with the tray was a struggle. The clatter had Mum there in a moment. She held the door for Sophie.

"You off now, love?" she asked.

"Where's she off to?" said Gran.

"Not yet. I'm going to do the washing-up first."

"There's no need," said Mum.

"No, really. I want to," said Sophie.

"Taken the hint, have you?" said Gran, peering over her glasses. Knitting needles clacked as the fluffy pink garment grew bigger.

"What hint?" asked Mum. Gran ignored Mum's question.

"I haven't done any washing-up at all since I've been upstairs," said Sophie. "I wouldn't want Gran to get the wrong impression."

"One of the compensations for being confined to your room," said Mum. There was an irritated splutter from Gran.

"Dropped a stitch?" asked Sophie, making an effort to be pleasant.

"Wouldn't you just like it if I had!" snapped Gran.

Sophie turned her attention to the dishes in the sink. Mum's hands pressed on her shoulders and steered her to the door.

"I don't want you to do the washing-up. Now buzz off and go to Emma's."

"But Mum . . ."

"There'll be plenty of other occasions when I shall be truly grateful. Right now I'm happy to do it myself." Sophie cast a glance at Gran. She appeared absorbed in her knitting pattern.

"Thanks, Mum," she said. "The casserole was great. See you later."

Once on the pavement Sophie had the feeling that it was warmer outside than in. Nevertheless she shivered. It was a grey dusk and would soon be dark. The street lights glowed orange on the leaves that had fallen from the plane tree. She shivered again and began to run along the pavement.

When she reached Emma's front door she looked back. Had she been followed? No. There was nothing there at all. She rang the bell. Footsteps came pounding along the hall, the door opened and Emma and Simon greeted her. Emma looked down the street, relieved to see everything was normal. Sophie grinned.

"Hello," she said.

Upstairs in Emma's room Sophie finally warmed up enough to take off her coat. Soon she was too hot and took off her sweater as well. She could hardly believe a bedroom could be so warm. They munched carob biscuits and drank fruit juice in comradely silence until Emma said through a mouthful, "Anything happened?"

"Nothing except my gran's getting suspicious."

"When's she going home?" asked Emma.

"That's the trouble," sighed Sophie. "She could be here for another whole week. Mum said so." Simon screwed up his nose.

"I'm glad our gran's not like that," he said.

"Simon!" said Emma.

"Well, I am." Sophie licked melted carob from her finger.

"That stuff's nice," she said.

"Not as nice as chocolate," said Emma.

"It is," said Simon.

"It's not."

"Come on, you two – don't start bickering. We've got to think about what to do. How are we going to get the boy here?"

"Has he still got the threepenny bit?" asked Emma.

"I don't know," said Sophie. "He might have left it on top of the wardrobe. I hadn't even thought of looking. But if it's not there I suppose he must have."

"We could do a sit-in in your room," suggested Simon. "Sooner or later he'll turn up."

"I left him a message," said Sophie. She explained about the PLEASE GET IN TOUCH note. "But he hasn't," she said.

In the end they decided to spend some time in Sophie's room the next day, as it was Saturday, and see what happened.

"We could always ask the witch," said Simon.

"I suppose you mean Mrs Russett?" said Emma.

"Good idea," said Sophie. "I bet she knows how to do it. I'll leave here early and pop in and ask her on my way home. We can start first thing in the morning."

Sophie left at half past eight. They agreed that half an hour should be plenty of time to talk to Mrs Russett. She didn't want to be late home and get into more trouble. As she walked by her house she looked up at her window. Her room seemed peaceful and quiet. The thirteen on the door was its usual dull-looking self. The house looked ordinary and like the others in the road. Sophie knocked on Mrs Russett's front door.

"Sophie!" said Mrs Russett. "Come in, dear. Come in." Mr Spiv and Gerty wandered into the hall to see who had arrived. Mr Spiv rubbed himself against Sophie's legs and rolled on to his back.

"Pleased to see you like I am," said Mrs Russett. She ushered Sophie into her back room. Met by the warmth, Sophie slipped out of her coat.

"Piece of toffee?"

"Yes, please," said Sophie.

"Now what can I do for you?" Mrs Russett inquired. "Any news?"

"The boy copied my essay for me," said Sophie through the toffee. Mrs Russett nodded. She listened as Sophie told her all about it and smiled.

"How kind," she said.

"I wish he'd come back. I'm sure he can help me find the key," said Sophie.

"Maybe he can and maybe he can't," said Mrs Russett. "But I think a note might be the wrong kind of message. He won't be able to read it. His is a different time with a different kind of writing. Not so many people could read and write then, you know."

"But the essay?"

"You said he copied it. He wouldn't necessarily have understood what he was copying."

"No," said Sophie. "I don't suppose he would."

"The thing to do is think threepenny bit," said Mrs Russett. "And think boy. He'll hear you."

"How can he hear what I'm thinking?"

"You'd be surprised," said Mrs Russett.

"All right," said Sophie. "I'll give it a go." She looked at the clock ticking steadily on Mrs Russett's mantlepiece. It said five to nine.

"I'd better go," she said. "Mum said home at nine and I don't want to make things worse. I'm in enough trouble with Gran as it is."

"I know, Sophie dear," said Mrs Russett. "Chalk and cheese. Doesn't mix, does it?"

Sophie slipped into her coat. She tickled Esmeralda behind the ears. Esmeralda lifted her head from her cushion appreciatively. Gerty was next. Sophie stroked the long fluffy hair of Gerty's back and tail.

"Me. Me too," miaowed Mr Spiv. Sophie scooped him up in her arms and gave him a big cuddle. Mr Spiv put his paws on her shoulder, nuzzled into her ear and purred.

"I wish I could take you home with me," said Sophie.

"Mr Spiv says he'd like to go with you but he wants to come back for his breakfast," said Mrs Russett.

"Mr Spiv, can I really take you home with me?" cried Sophie. "What would Mum say? And Gran – Gran would hate it. No, better not," said Sophie. Gently, she put Mr Spiv on the floor. "Not while Gran's there. Thank you for the toffee."

Mrs Russett waved to her as she set off along the pavement. Sophie's key went into the lock of number thirteen at exactly nine o'clock.

"That was well timed," said Mum as Sophie went into the kitchen. "Did you have a nice time?"

"Yes, thanks," said Sophie as she put the kettle on for her hot-water bottle. "Is it okay if Emma and Simon come round tomorrow?"

"Of course," said Mum.

"I hope you're going to behave yourselves." Gran's voice sounded sharp. "We don't want a repetition of last weekend, do we?" Sophie made for the door.

"I'll bring your bottle up," said Mum.

Before she got into bed Sophie looked on top of the wardrobe. There was nothing there. The threepenny bit had vanished with the boy. Shivering, she climbed into bed. At last Mum came in with the hot-water bottle. Sophie gratefully clasped it to her.

"Night, night," said Mum, giving her a kiss. "Goodness, this room *is* cold. It seems colder than anywhere else in the house."

"It is," said Sophie. She was already half asleep. Mum crept out and shut the door behind her.

It was about ten o'clock the next morning when Emma and Simon arrived at number thirteen. Sophie ushered them upstairs as quickly as she could. She had been waiting for them for ages. As soon as her bedroom door was shut Emma asked, "Did you find out what to do?"

"Yep! It's easy. All we've got to do is . . ." Sophie didn't finish. A scrabbling at the window caused her to turn sharply to see what it was.

"Mr Spiv!" she cried. Mr Spiv stood on the windowsill and miaowed.

"He wants to come in," said Emma.

Sophie opened the window and Mr Spiv jumped to the floor. She stroked him, then wriggled a frayed end of the rug and Mr Spiv pounced.

"He must have climbed the tree and jumped," said Simon, impressed. Emma closed the window.

"You still haven't said what we've got to do."

"We've got to think threepenny bit and think boy."

"What?" Emma raised her eyes to the ceiling. "That's not going to do much, is it? Not unless he's a mind reader or something." Sophie shrugged.

"That's what Mrs Russett said."

"Let's do it then," said Simon. "It'll work."

"How do you know?" said Emma.

"I just do. We should stand in a circle and hold hands when we do it," he said.

"Come on – let's start," said Sophie.

Reluctantly Emma took hold of the proffered hands.

"Okay," said Sophie. "Let's think."

"We've got to imagine too," said Simon.

"Yes, that's it. Think and imagine," said Sophie. She and Simon closed their eyes and began. Reluctantly, Emma followed suit. None of them noticed Mr Spiv slip between their legs and enter the middle of the circle. He sat, his green eyes staring and still as though he too were thinking.

They must have been like that for a minute or two. It seemed like ages to Emma. Her concentration went and she began to fidget. Sophie opened her eyes. Mr Spiv brushed himself against her legs and walked to the window.

"I think the boy's got the message," said Simon.

"How do you know?" Emma asked.

"I just know."

Sophie broke the circle and opened the window. Mr Spiv leapt on to the sill with a bound and with another he was in the tree.

"That's odd, isn't it? He's never come up here before. How did he know where to come?" said Sophie.

"Mrs Russett sent him, I bet," said Simon.

"You could be right." Sophie watched Mr Spiv jump from the tree on to the pavement before closing the window.

"Well," she said. "I suppose all we can do now is wait."

Emma was already sitting hunched up on the bed. Sophie and Simon joined her. Time seemed ages in the passing. Suddenly Simon stiffened. Sophie leaned forward. A gentle hissing began. A long crack of green light appeared on the carpet. The three of them watched. Slowly the crack of light grew. A huge shadow arched along the wall as though a great door were opening. Green light filled the room and he was there. Sophie could see him. He held up his hand in salute.

Simon, as if bidden, got off the bed and walked towards him. Too late Sophie saw the white tentacles pass the boy and wrap themselves around Simon. The wispy boy held up his hands as if surprised. The tentacles formed into a great height. Things in the room began to move. The curtains swayed towards the great door as the hooded creature they had seen before pushed Simon forward towards the source of the light. The figure turned.

"The boy for the key!" it hissed.

Sophie and Emma were frozen to the bed. The arched shadow moved along the wall and disappeared as the green light narrowed. The door swung shut with a hiss. Simon had gone. The curtains swayed into stillness. A threepenny bit fell from the air and landed with a thud on the carpet. Emma screamed.

Chapter Eleven

Mum and Gran, summoned by Emma's scream, wanted to know what was wrong. Emma blurted it out through her tears.

"What do you mean 'Simon's disappeared'?" Mum asked. "There, there, Emma. You've been in here all morning, haven't you?"

"Yes," said Sophie. She wished everyone would go away so that she could concentrate. "The boy for the key," she thought. "They've taken him as hostage." She hoped Simon would be all right.

Mum asked Emma to say exactly what had happened as she was the one who seemed the most upset. Emma was too distraught. Mum turned to Sophie.

"Don't worry Mum. It's only a temporary disappearance. He'll be back soon." Sophie tried to sound confident. Inside she didn't feel it in the least. If only Emma hadn't screamed.

"That doesn't tell us much," said Gran.

"Is that the best you can do?" asked Mum.

"Yes, well, it's like he's just popped out for a bit," said Sophie.

"Popped out where?" said Gran. "Has the boy gone out or hasn't he? That's a simple enough question, isn't it?"

"He has and he hasn't," said Sophie. "It's difficult to explain."

"They've had a row, that's what," said Gran. "Plain as houses. Though I can't understand why Madam here can't explain things without making a big mystery of it."

"Did you have a row?" Mum asked. Sophie caught the look of panic in Emma's eye.

"You could say there's been a bit of a disagreement," she said.

"Something you can sort out amongst yourselves?"

"Oh, yes," said Sophie. "Yes, I'm sure we can."

"All right then," said Mum. "We'll leave you to it. Are you sure you're all right, Emma?"

Emma nodded not trusting herself to speak. She lowered her eyes. Something on the floor caught her attention. The threepenny bit was floating a little way above the carpet. Sophie saw it too. She stepped between the threepenny bit and Mum and Gran so that they couldn't see it. Emma bit her lip.

"I'll pop up later and see how you're getting on," said Mum. "If I were you I'd make it up with Simon. He *is* younger than you, don't forget." With that she closed the door.

"I'm sorry I screamed. I'm sorry," said Emma. "What are we going to do?"

"He's here. The boy," said Sophie. "He's going to help us. I know he didn't mean Simon to be kidnapped."

"It's awful!" said Emma. "Awful. What'll happen if we can't get him back."

"We will," said Sophie. "They won't keep him for long."

The threepenny bit hovered in the air and came down on Sophie's table. She could make out the outline of the boy.

"Emma, can you see him?"

"No. Where are we going to look for this key?" Sophie turned to the boy.

"Where shall we look for the key, please?" she asked. The boy stayed by the table. Sophie shivered. His presence seemed to make the room colder. She thought back to the dream image she had had at Mrs Russett's. She remembered the tunnel and the studded door. It was a passageway to a dungeon. The key on a high ledge out of reach. A big iron key.

"A dungeon. Of course! It must have been below here," she cried.

Emma blew her nose and shoved her soggy tissue in her pocket. She had absorbed the shock of Simon's going and was ready for action to get him back.

"What are you on about?" said Emma. "We've got to get moving and fast. What happens if my parents find out Simon has disappeared? We won't get away with that kind of explanation again. Your mum wasn't convinced anyway."

"Don't you see?" said Sophie. "The castle that was here must have had a dungeon. That's where the key is. That's where I saw it in my head."

"That's all very well but how are we going to find it?" asked Emma.

"There's only one place to start looking and that's the cellar."

"The cellar!" said Emma.

"Yes, don't you see? Dungeons were dug out of the ground. Castles were built on top of their dungeons. We've got to go down. Dig down if we have to."

"What happens if we find your gran in the cellar?"

"We won't," said Sophie. "Let's think. We'll need some light. I've got a small torch and there are some candles in the kitchen if we can get them." Sophie beckoned to the boy. "Hey, are you coming?"

She picked up the torch from the floor beside her bed. As she and Emma moved towards the door the shadowy boy began to follow them. On the landing they heard the sound of voices coming from Mum's bedroom. They were in luck. They crept downstairs as silently as they could. Emma waited in the hall while Sophie nipped into the kitchen to fetch the candles. The voices could be heard on the landing now. They were raised in disagreement. Sophie came out of the kitchen and Emma pointed urgently above her head. Sophie dived for the door under the stairs that led down to the cellar. Emma followed close behind. They closed the door as Mum and Gran arrived at the bottom of the stairs.

"Look, Mum, I expect they've gone to find Simon to make it up. Sophie's not the monster you make her out to be. You don't give her a chance."

"If that's the way you feel about it there's nothing more to be said." The kitchen door slammed.

"Phew!" whispered Sophie. "They must have come out of Mum's room and gone into mine."

"We just made it," Emma whispered.

They were standing in gloom. What light there was came from gaps around the edge of the door. The stairs were pitch black. Sophie switched on the torch. She gasped. A boy's face stared at her from below then turned and disappeared down the steps.

"Did you see him?" Sophie asked. Emma shook her head.

"Can't we put the light on?" she asked.

"No," whispered Sophie. "The hall's dark enough for it to show. We'll have enough light with the torch."

Shining the torch ahead Sophie started down the steps. Emma followed. They turned the bend at the bottom. Sophie played the beam of light around the cellar. It wasn't big and for a cellar it wasn't damp, but it was cold. There wasn't much in it either, just the bottles that Gran had rummaged through and odd bits of junk left by previous occupants of the house. It was hard to tell what they were – an old bedhead, the bottom half of a standard lamp – useless stuff.

"Shine the torch here," said Emma. The light slid along the floor. Emma picked up a rusty iron bar. "This might be useful," she said.

"Hang on to it then," Sophie said. She shone the torch around the walls, looking for a likely way through. The walls looked solid and strong. They weren't stone as Sophie had thought they would be. They were brick.

"This cellar was built with the house," said Emma.

"I'm going to light some candles. Can you hold the torch?" said Sophie.

She dragged the bedhead into the middle of the floor and lay it flat. She took two candles out of the box and struck a match. She lit one candle and with it melted the bottom of the other. She stuck it to the bedhead. She lit it and stuck the one she was holding next to it. Soon they had the light of two candles to see by. They burned steadily with upright flames that barely flickered.

"If there was any kind of doorway," said Emma, "there should be a draught and the flames should flicker."

"I know," said Sophie.

Emma put the torch in her pocket and began to tap the bricks with the iron bar. Not too hard, so they wouldn't be heard upstairs, but hard enough to see if they sounded hollow. They didn't. Bits of crumbling mortar fell to the floor.

"This must be the way," said Sophie. "But I don't see how."

"Neither do I," said Emma. She stopped tapping.

Sophie sat on the bottom step. Emma joined her. Sophie put her hand on the step beneath her and jumped as though it had given her a shock.

"I wish you wouldn't do that," said Emma. "My heart's just skipped a beat."

"It's stone," said Sophie. "Don't you see? The steps to here are wooden. This is stone. The walls are brick and this is stone."

"No, I don't see," said Emma.

"The floor's stone too!"

"It's a flagstone floor but they're laid on earth, I expect," said Emma.

"But they might not be," said Sophie. "Stone steps will go down to the dungeon." Emma looked doubtful.

"I don't think that proves anything," Emma said. All the same she took the iron bar and tapped across the flagstones. They sounded solid and not the least bit hollow. She sat down again.

"I know this is right," said Sophie, clenching her fists. "I just know it is."

"Do you think we should try lifting a flagstone?" Emma asked.

"We could, I suppose," said Sophie. "But which one? Where's the most likely spot?"

They stared at the floor. The area wasn't huge. Nevertheless, the flagstones were big and they looked heavy. It was going to take a lot of effort to move one.

"I wonder if the boy would know which one we should try," said Sophie.

"Can you see him?"

"No, he's not here."

"Let's think for him," Emma said.

They stood up and held hands. They closed their eyes and concentrated. After what seemed like ages the candle flames flickered. Sophie opened her eyes. Light played on the walls as the flames darted. Emma opened her eyes in surprise.

"A draught. Where's it coming from?"

From almost beneath their feet the head of the boy appeared. The rest of him followed as if he were coming up a staircase. He stood in front of them, his pale face set in a stare. He pointed downwards, then turned and walked through the wall.

"Did you see?" cried Sophie. "It's here!"

"Where?"

"The boy came up here," said Sophie. She jumped on the flagstone. Nothing happened. But when she spread her feet and moved from side to side she felt a shift in the stone.

"We've got to get this one up," she said.

Emma tried pushing the iron bar into the crack between the stones. She heaved this way and that but she couldn't push it down.

"We've got to get the bar down the side here so we can lever the stone up," she gasped.

"We need something to bash it with," said Sophie. "Like a nice heavy hammer which we haven't got.

97

Great!" Sophie looked around the cellar in vain.
"Mum's got a small hammer but it would be
useless." They sat on the stone step in despair. "Who
do you know who's got the right sort of hammer?"

"Mum and Dad might have," said Emma. "But it
would mean going home to get it."

"It's the only way we're going to get the flagstone
up," said Sophie.

The candle flames flickered sending shadows
swaying across the floor. A hammer appeared before
them. Sophie and Emma ducked out of the way. The
hammer dropped with some force on to the flagstone.

"I don't know where you got it from, but thank
you!" said Sophie to thin air. She picked up the
hammer. It was heavy.

"You hold the bar in place and I'll hit it," she
ordered.

"You'd better not miss, that's all," said Emma.

Emma held the bar on the crack, her hands well
down, and gritted her teeth. Sophie raised the
hammer above her head and brought it down with all
the force she could muster. It hit the bar, metal on
metal. The bar stayed upright, wedged between the
flagstones. Sophie hit it again and again until it was
well down. Emma leaned against the bar with all her
weight. Sophie joined her. Slowly the stone lifted.
Sophie jammed the hammer under it. They moved
the bar to the other end and heaved. The flagstone
lifted up and out. With much puffing and panting
they pulled it out of the way.

Sophie stabbed the place where it had been with
the iron bar. She dug and dug. Without any warning
the bar went through the earth and Sophie would
have fallen but for Emma grabbing her.

"I've gone through!" she gasped. Emma took the

bar from Sophie and pushed the earth into the hole, enlarging it as she did so. Earth clattered on to stone below. Soon the hole was big enough to squeeze through. Emma got out the torch and Sophie lit another candle. They looked at the hole and glanced at one another.

"Come on," said Sophie. "I'll go first." The hole looked black and uninviting. Swallowing a butterfly feeling, Sophie swung her legs down, felt for a foothold and went below.

Chapter Twelve

Once through the hole and standing firm on a stone step Sophie held up her candle. She was sure this was what she had seen in the dream at Mrs Russett's. There was a stale, musty smell of old air. She called up to Emma.

"It's fine! There are steps. It's quite safe."

Emma put her feet through the hole and found herself beside Sophie, looking down to a stone passageway.

"This is it," Sophie said.

"It smells," said Emma.

"No ventilation," said Sophie. They climbed to the bottom of the steps, Sophie's candle lighting the way. The passageway seemed long but this may have been because they travelled it slowly. Moving cautiously Emma shone the torch ahead and they saw the passageway bend. They went around the bend with their backs to the wall, alert for danger. Emma pointed the torch. Ahead of them they saw it – the tall studded door and, up on a ledge, the key.

"It's there!" said Emma.

"I can see it," said Sophie. "Why hasn't the boy taken it?"

"Perhaps he doesn't want the door locked," said Emma.

"Then why show us where the key is?" said Sophie.

"I don't know. Maybe he's sorry for Simon or something," said Emma.

"Or maybe he can't get it. But we can. Come on. If you lean against the wall, I'll climb on to your shoulders. I should be able to reach it from there."

Sophie put her candle on the ground. She jumped on to Emma's back and pulled herself up by squeezing her fingers into the stonework above Emma's head. Emma grunted.

"Sorry," said Sophie. She had a foot on either shoulder. Feeling upwards she could reach the bottom of the ledge but only just. She put her hands over the ledge, pushed off from Emma with her feet and scrabbled upwards. Letting go with one hand she grabbed the key and slithered down the wall, ending in a heap on the floor. There was a distant rumbling.

"Quick!" said Sophie, scrambling up. "Quick! Get out of here."

The two of them fled down the passageway, leaving the candle on the ground, Emma with the torch, Sophie with the key. The key was surprisingly heavy. There was a cracking behind them and stones fell from the ceiling. They clambered up the steps and crawled into the cellar. A rumbling followed them as they lay panting on the floor. Slowly a cloud of dust seeped out of the hole. Emma began to cough. Sophie pulled the old bedhead over it and piled some

101

more junk on top, snuffing out the candles in the process.

"Come on," she said. "Let's get out of here."

As they climbed the cellar steps the ground beneath them began to shake. The rumbling grew into a thunderous roar.

"Quick!" said Sophie. "My room!"

They burst out of the cellar door and met Gran. Her eyes were alight with fury.

"Meddlesome children!" she shrieked. "You'll have the house down about our ears!"

Sophie didn't wait to hear more. She pushed past and Emma followed. They pelted upstairs.

"Wait till I tell your mother about this!" yelled Gran. "When she gets back from shopping I'll tell her."

At the top of the stairs Sophie turned. Gran raged in the hall, her hair sticking out as straight as giant matchsticks.

"She's mad!" gasped Emma.

They ran into Sophie's room. Sophie flung the key on to her bed and bolted the door. She rammed her chair under the door handle.

"Quick, help me with this." Sophie and Emma hauled the chest of drawers across the floor and pushed it against the door. They were just in time. The door handle turned. Gran banged loudly when she found the door locked.

"You wait, you minx! You wait! I'll have you sent to an orphanage for this. You . . . you disobedient, uncooperative, rebellious incompetent."

Emma's eyes were startled and wild.

"You're right," said Sophie. "She's mad." She picked up the key. "Hold hands and think tall, cloaked being," she said. She put the key between them. "And think key."

There was silence. The rumbling had stopped. Somewhere in the house a door banged. It sounded like Gran's. They concentrated. The thinking calmed them and their breathing slowed.

"Tall, cloaked being," whispered Sophie. "We have the key."

Sophie and Emma stayed in the summoning position until persistent miaows and scratching came from the window and distracted them.

"It's Mr Spiv!" cried Sophie, rushing to the window to let the cat in. He sprang lightly to the floor. Without more ado he trotted to the bed, jumped up and sat washing himself expectantly. Sophie picked up the key. She and Emma joined Mr Spiv on the bed. They too were expectant. The hissing began. Mr Spiv's coat crackled as though full of electricity. He hissed too, his hackles rising. Sophie clasped the key tightly in her lap. She liked the large teeth, the solidness of it. Some blacksmith long ago had forged it. She felt a momentary pang at having to give it up.

Mr Spiv hissed at the green crack that appeared on the floor. They watched as the door swung open, slowly flooding the room with eerie light. The energy began. The curtains were lifted from the wall. Paper slid from the table. Sophie stood up. Holding tight to the key she took a step forward. Mr Spiv darted in front of her and hissed.

"Go back!" he seemed to say. "Go back!"

Sophie obeyed. With effort she stepped backwards and found herself pulled on to the bed by Emma. Mr Spiv tried to jump up beside them. The sucking wind pulled him down. He clung to the bedspread with his claws and was rescued by Emma who clasped him to

103

her. The pulling slowed. Sophie watched as the threepenny bit fell from the table and rolled across the rug. Wispy tentacles covered it. They swirled high and formed the tall hooded being.

"The key!" it hissed.

Sophie stood and held out the key. The being towered above her. Sophie felt a force pull at the key and let it go.

"Where's Simon?" she asked. "You said you'd give him back."

"So I shall," hissed the being.

"There's the boy," said Sophie. "Don't leave him on this side."

The threepenny bit hovered in the air and vanished.

"What boy?" hissed the being. But the boy and the threepenny bit had gone.

"Please give us Simon," said Sophie.

"Simon is yours. A bargain is a bargain."

The hooded figure retreated into the green light. The door began to close. The shadow of the key meeting the keyhole impressed itself on the wall for a brief moment. The door slammed shut. The room shook violently.

"Where's Simon?" yelled Emma, as the three of them were flung to the floor. The bed, the chair and the chest of drawers slid forwards. The bolt snapped on the door. It swung open. At the same time there was a rending of bricks and mortar from the outside wall and the window panes shattered. Glass flew everywhere. From somewhere above them came a thunderous crash, followed by a loud scream and the sound of falling masonry. Slowly the house settled into stillness. Mr Spiv shook himself and gave himself a lick.

"Don't let him walk on the glass," said Sophie. But Mr Spiv made no move to go.

"I want Simon," sobbed Emma.

"He must be here," said Sophie. "Let's go and look for him."

She grabbed Emma by the hand. Mr Spiv ran ahead. Sophie pulled the sobbing Emma after him. He led them past Gran's room and up the stairs to the attic room. As they reached the attic door it swung open. Simon's pale face stared down at them.

"Hello," he said.

Emma flung herself at him. She half-pulled him out of the attic and looked him over.

"Are you all right?" she asked. "Are you?"

"Yes, I'm fine." Simon seemed surprised at all the fuss.

"Where've you been?" asked Sophie.

"I've been up here all the time," said Simon. "I was gagged so I couldn't shout. I had manacles on my wrists and a ball and chain round my ankles so I couldn't move either. Just now the chains fell off. I've undone the gag. Did you find the key?" Sophie nodded.

"The thing is, when the ball and chain fell off it crashed through the ceiling. I think your mum's going to be pretty mad."

Sophie remembered the scream.

"Gran!" she gasped. She ran along the landing and knocked at Gran's door.

"What do you want?" Gran's voice was sharp. Sophie let out a breath of relief. She opened the door, Emma and Simon behind her. They stared. Bits of plaster were everywhere. The room was a dreadful mess.

"You've achieved what you wanted, Sophie.

Everything ruined. I can't stand it a minute longer. I'm off. Your mother'll have to pay. I'm not."

"But Gran . . ." Sophie began.

"An accident, was it?" snapped Gran. "A fine kind of accident. I could have been killed."

"We didn't do it."

"Pull the other one."

"We didn't," said Sophie. "Honestly, it wasn't our fault."

"Oh, get out! Get out all of you!" yelled Gran. She pushed them out. "And leave me in peace." She slammed the door. More plaster cascaded to the floor.

"We'd better find Mum," said Sophie. "This is going to take some explaining."

On the way downstairs Simon looked in through Sophie's open door.

"Crumbs!" he said. "How did it happen?" The room was in chaos.

"Well," said Sophie, "it's a long story."

Mr Spiv ran past them and down the stairs. He miaowed by the front door to be let out. Sophie ran and opened it. She met Mum on the doorstep. Mr Spiv trotted out. Mum didn't even notice a cat had been in the house.

"Come outside, all of you," she ordered. "Where's Gran?"

"Upstairs," said Sophie.

"You stay on the pavement. I'm going to fetch her. I don't know how it's happened but the house is wrecked." Mum threw this shattering statement over her shoulder and rushed upstairs.

"Better do what she says," said Sophie.

There was quite a crowd in the street. Sophie wondered what all the fuss was about. Something odd had happened to the front path. It had gone crooked.

"Heck!" said Emma. "Look at that!"

The pavement, outside the house, was a mass of cracked and upturned paving stones. The plane tree was leaning at a lopsided angle. But even that wasn't what everyone was staring at. They were looking at the house. Sophie looked too and saw a crack, several inches wide, stretch upward from above the front door, past her window, to the roof. Her bedroom window was lopsided and dislodged tiles were caught in the gutter, looking as if they might fall at any minute.

"That's incredible," she said.

"Do you think the house'll collapse?" asked Simon.

"I don't know. It doesn't look very safe, does it?" An old man tapped Sophie on the shoulder.

"You've had a lucky escape, my girl," he said. "I've not seen anything like that since the Blitz."

"A bad case of subsidence, that's what that is," said a woman. "Monstrous, isn't it, that innocent people should live in a place like that? Should be condemned, that's what."

"It will be now," remarked the old man. "No one could live in that."

Two bags of shopping were leaning against the wall.

"Mum's," thought Sophie.

It was with some relief that Sophie saw Mrs Russett coming along the pavement. She smiled when she saw Sophie.

"Don't worry, dear, I've called the police. They'll know what to do." She put her arm round Sophie's shoulder. "There," she said under her breath. "I told

107

you you could do it. Well done! It's a shame it's made such a mess. Not much we can do about that, is there?"

"No," said Sophie. "There isn't."

Mum, stoney-faced, appeared in the doorway carrying Gran's suitcase. Gran followed her into the street.

"I tell you it was them," Gran raged, pointing at the three children. "They did it."

"Don't talk rubbish, woman!" scoffed the old man. "Not even a horde of children could do that." He pointed at the crack.

"I tell you they did!" Gran snarled. "I want a taxi!" she snapped at Mum. "And you needn't expect a visit from me again. Not after this." She stared at her chipped nail varnish in anguish and patted her coat sleeve. Dust billowed out. "Ruined!" she muttered. "Absolutely ruined. Well! What about my taxi?"

"Mum, Mrs Russett's phoned for the police," said Sophie.

"They'll know what to do," said Mrs Russett. "And I took the liberty of phoning for a taxi too. Here it is." Mum gave Mrs Russett a curious glance.

The sound of the police siren could be heard approaching but the taxi arrived first. It cruised down the street and drew up outside number thirteen. Gran climbed in. Mum struggled after her with the suitcase. The taxi driver took it.

"Here, love," he said. "I'll do that." He put the case in the boot. Mum waved as the taxi drove off. Gran stared straight ahead and ignored her.

"She's horrid!" said Simon under his breath. "A real nasty." Emma nudged him to be quiet.

Sophie looked at Mum. She saw tears in Mum's

eyes and a lump came into her own throat.

"The police will tell us what to do," said Sophie, giving Mum's hand a squeeze. Mum squeezed back.

"And then you must come to my house," said Mrs Russett. "For tea. Good for shocked nerves. I'm going to put the kettle on now."

Chapter Thirteen

Mum sat back wearily in the armchair sipping a cup of tea. She had listened to the story told by Sophie, Emma and Simon and found it hard to believe. Yet the evidence collected by the police – the ball and chain and the manacles, both found in Gran's room – and the caved-in hole in the cellar made it difficult to dismiss the story out of hand. Besides, she knew Sophie to be a truthful child and Mrs Russett believed it too. Altogether it was quite extraordinary.

"There've been problems at number thirteen for years," said Mrs Russett. "People have come and gone. The disturbances have caused many a grey hair."

"Do you remember the face you saw at the kitchen window?" Sophie asked. Mum nodded. She remembered. She thought she had imagined it. At the time she told herself not to be silly. Had it been real after all?

"That was the boy," said Sophie.

"You know, I think we should keep this part of the story under our hats," said Mrs Russett.

"So do I," said Mum. "No one's going to believe it."

"Let people think it a straightforward case of house subsidence," said Mrs Russett, "caused by the collapse of the old passageway upsetting the foundations. That's what any report will say."

"That does seem the best thing to do," said Mum. "We'll have less fuss that way. The police have warned me to expect reporters."

"Reporters?" said Sophie and Emma together. Their eyes lit up.

"Will we be on television?" Simon asked.

"Goodness knows," said Mum. She began fishing in her handbag for her purse. She put down her cup and stood up.

"Where you going, Mum?" Sophie asked.

"To telephone a hotel. I'm afraid we can't stay in the house – it's too unsafe."

"I won't hear of a hotel," said Mrs Russett. "You're to stay here. I thought I'd already said. My memory's not what it was. I've plenty of space and besides, I've got the beds airing."

Mum looked as though she was going to protest. Then she sat down and said thank you. Sophie was overjoyed.

"Can Mr Spiv sleep on my bed?" she asked.

Mum was about to say no when Mrs Russett said, "Mr Spiv sleeps where he chooses."

"Mr Spiv," said Sophie. "Please, feel free to choose my bed." She stroked his ears. He purred. Gerty, not wanting to be left out, came over to be stroked too. "And you too, Gerty. You can sleep on my bed any time you like." Gerty looked as if she

111

would like. Her eyes took on a faraway look as Sophie tickled her chin.

Mum said she would go and pack their things. Sophie said she would come too. But Mum, with a gentle firmness, said no, she wasn't taking any chances. Sophie had been in enough danger as it was. So the three children waited outside number thirteen with the onlookers and a policeman.

They were sitting on the front path when a man in a suit tapped Emma on the shoulder.

"Are you the child who lives here?" he asked. The man was abrasive and, Emma felt, rude. She didn't reply. Sophie's face screwed into its famous frown.

"Who wants her?" she asked.

"I do," said the man.

"Who are you?" said Sophie.

The man looked irritated. Clearly he expected everyone to jump to it when he asked questions. Sophie could almost see him thinking "what revolting children!" She didn't care. Emma grinned encouragingly at Sophie from behind the man's back. His unpleasant manner didn't warrant a pleasant response and Sophie was quite prepared to match unpleasantness with unpleasantness. Simon, not such a rebel, got up to go.

"Perhaps I can get some sense from the little boy," said the man. "What's your name?"

"Simon," said Simon, and walked off leaving the man standing there.

A woman with a video camera slung on her shoulder was grinning at them from the pavement, obviously enjoying the man's discomfort.

"Look," he said, "I've come to do an interview for the local television news. I want to get some sense out of someone." Sophie carried on frowning.

112

"If this is television," she thought, "they can stuff it!"

"Hi, kids!" said a man in jeans and a sloppy sweater waiting by the gate. "I see you've already met our intrepid roving reporter."

The man in the suit narrowed his eyes.

"I can't get a word out of them," he said stiffly.

"What a surprise!" said the man in jeans. "Would you like to give us an interview?" he asked. "You were inside the house when it shifted, weren't you?" Sophie nodded and looked at Emma. Emma shrugged.

"Why not?" she said.

"All right," said Sophie.

"Don't overdo the enthusiasm," said the man in jeans, pulling a face at them.

"Do I have to talk to him?" asked Sophie, jerking her thumb at the man in the suit.

"I'm afraid you do," the man in jeans said. Sophie thought about it.

"Okay," she said.

That was how it came to be that Sophie Bartholomew was seen on the television with her famous frown. She didn't say much and kept quiet about the ball and chain.

The newspaper reporter was much nicer and all three children chatted away to her. She kept saying, "gosh!" and "golly!" and "that must have been scary" as she scribbled away in her notebook. Sophie even told her about the ball and chain.

"A ball and chain?" said the reporter.

"It fell through the ceiling," said Sophie. "It's ever so old."

That was how the woman from the museum came to hear about the Norman relics found at number thirteen, Castle Street. She read it in the *Snareswick Echo*.

"Oh dear," said Mum when Sophie told her about the television people and the reporter. "I hope you didn't say anything about well, you know . . ."

"Mum!" said Sophie. "Would I? But I did say about the ball and chain."

"I can't see any harm in that," said Mum. "After all, that is real."

"Hold it!" called a man's voice. Sophie frowned.

"Now what?" she said. There was a flash.

"Photograph for the newspaper," said the man. That was how Sophie's famous frown appeared in the newspaper.

They watched the television news at Emma and Simon's house. Mum sighed when she saw Sophie's face. Emma's mum, a solicitor, was so shocked by the report that she took up the case.

"The landlord ought to be sued," she said. "You might have been killed." Sophie wondered how anyone could have known the building was going to crack.

All Emma's dad would say was, "I think it worth pursuing. All right with you, Ann?"

"If you think so," said Mum. "Yes."

Mrs Russett bought the newspaper. The headline read SENSATION IN CASTLE STREET.

"I suppose it was quite sensational," said Mum. She shuddered. "Thank goodness that the whole house didn't crumble."

On Sunday the woman from the museum traced them to Mrs Russett's house and knocked at the door. Mum took her to number thirteen and showed her the ball and chain and the manacles. She stroked them with awe.

114

"They shouldn't be left lying around," she said. She lifted the manacles. "It's as if they were made yesterday. I've never seen anything of such quality." She helped Mum carry them to the front door.

When Emma and Simon came round, Sophie and Mum asked them to help carry the ball and chain and manacles to Mrs Russett's. They hid them under the front room sofa. It took quite an effort as the ball was very heavy.

"Dad said he'll get them valued for you if you like. They could be worth a fortune," said Emma.

When Sophie came home from school on Monday, cheered by all the attention her fame had brought her, she was greeted by Mrs Russett's smiling face.

"Hello, Sophie dear. Nice day at school?"

"Very nice, thank you," said Sophie, swinging her school bag from her shoulder and dumping it on the hall floor. Then, thinking that Mrs Russett might not like such behaviour, she went to pick it up again. Mrs Russett didn't appear to mind in the slightest. So in the end she left it.

"Got much homework?" Mrs Russett asked.

"Not much," said Sophie.

"Good," said Mrs Russett. "That means we can have a cosy evening together in front of the fire."

They went into the back room, where Sophie was surprised to find Mum sitting hunched in an armchair.

"Hello, Mum! You're back early," she said.

"I got the sack."

"You got the sack!" Sophie didn't know whether to laugh or cry. Deep down she felt pleased. From inside welled a cheer so she let it out.

"Hooray!" she cried.

"Sophie, this is serious," Mum said. "Mr Smart said he wasn't having an employee who brought sensational publicity to the firm."

"Can't think why," said Mrs Russett. "They say publicity's good for business, don't they?"

"I think it was an excuse," said Mum. "He's never liked me."

"But think how he's going to miss you. He's never noticed how hard you worked," said Sophie.

"Serve him right, then!" said Mrs Russett.

"But what are we going to do?" Mum said. "I'll have to start looking for a new job tomorrow. I've never had the sack before. Do I have to tell people that?"

"Stop, stop, stop!" said Mrs Russett. Mum stopped. "What a lot of worrying nonsense! You're safe and sound with me now. What you need is a holiday, not another job."

"Hear, hear!" said Sophie. "I agree. It's half term next week. We could go somewhere together."

"Excellent idea," said Mrs Russett. "Piece of toffee, Sophie?"

Even Mum took a piece.

"Nice, isn't it?" said Sophie, chewing hard.

"Mmm," said Mum. "Very nice." As she chewed she pondered. "Maybe you're right," she said at last. "We could do with a holiday. I'm sure things will turn out all right in the end."

And they did. Emma's mum came to a satisfactory arrangement with the landlord of number thirteen, who felt some remorse at letting the house in the first place, knowing its reputation. This included being allowed to keep the ball and chain and the manacles.

"Whatever shall we do with them?" said Mum

"Sell them and make our fortune," suggested Sophie.

"I suppose we could," said Mum.

When Mum and Sophie came back from their holiday Mrs Russett asked them to stay for good.

"You mean for always?" cried Sophie, who couldn't think of anything nicer. She longed to tell the ghost boy how he had helped to make things turn out so well.

"Well, if you're sure," said Mum, who was looking happy for the first time Sophie could remember. "Thank you."

"That's settled then," said Mrs Russett, pleased. "It's so nice having young people about the house. It's given my old bones a fair old shake-up. Just what they needed." Mrs Russett too was feeling a sense of satisfaction at the way things had turned out.

There came a time when Mum's happy face faded and Sophie knew at once who she was thinking about – Gran.

"I'll write to her," said Mum.

"She'll come round in the end," said Mrs Russett. "She'll see she was over-hasty in her judgement. Even us old 'uns have things to learn."

"I hope so," said Mum.

"I'll write too, shall I?" said Sophie.

"Will you, Sophie?" said Mum. "We can send the letters together."

That night in her room, sitting at the table that Mrs Russett had arranged for her, with Mr Spiv and Gerty curled up on her bed and the gas fire glowing in the hearth, Sophie felt full of joy. She acknowledged the misunderstandings and the differences between her and Gran and felt forgiving. She didn't know if she'd always feel that way but she decided to try. Besides, the letter was done.

"And now", she said to her sleepy audience, "I shall write to Skinny Tim." What a letter it was going to be! She picked up her pen. Then it dawned on her. Skinny was most likely to say he didn't believe a word of it.

"Well, I shall tell him just the same. He can believe it or not." And she began to write:

Dear Skinny Tim,

Guess what? I've been haunted . . .

HIPPO BESTSELLERS

You'll find loads of very popular Hippo books to suit all tastes.
You'll be in stitches with our joke books, enthralled with our
adventure stories, in love with our romances, amazed at our
non-fiction titles and kept amused for hours with all our
activity books. Here are just a few of our most popular titles:

A Dark Dark Tale (picture book) by Ruth Brown   £1.95
Postman Pat Goes Sledging by John Cunliffe   £1.75
Little Tiger Get Well Soon (picture book) by Janosch   £1.95
Bambi (picture book) by The Walt Disney Company   £1.75
The Ghostbusters Story Book by Anne Digby   £2.50
Cry Vampire (fiction) by Terrance Dicks   £1.50
Nellie and the Dragon (fiction) by Elizabeth Lindsay   £1.75
Aliens in the Family (fiction) by Margaret Mahy   £1.50
Voices (fiction) by Joan Aiken   £1.95
Cheerleaders Summer Special (fiction)   £2.95
My First Christmas Activity Book
by Donna Bryant   £2.50
Sleuth (activity) by Sherlock Ransford   £1.50
Modern Disasters (non-fiction) by Jane Ferguson   £1.95
The Spooktacular Joke Book by Theodore Freek   £1.25
Stupid Cupid (joke book) by Trudie Hart   £1.75

You'll find these and many more great Hippo books at your
local bookshop, or you can order them direct. Just send off to
*Customer Services, Hippo Books, Westfield Road, Southam,
Leamington Spa, Warwickshire CV33 0JH*, not forgetting to
enclose a cheque or postal order for the price of the book(s)
plus 30p per book for postage and packing.

HAUNTINGS by Hippo Books is a new series of excellent ghost stories for older readers.

Ghost Abbey by Robert Westall
When Maggie and her family move into a run-down old abbey, they begin to notice some very strange things going on in the rambling old building. Is there any truth in the rumour that the abbey is haunted?

Don't Go Near the Water by Carolyn Sloan
Brendan knew instinctively that he shouldn't go near Blackwater Lake. Especially that summer, when the water level was so low. But what was the dark secret that lurked in the depths of the lake?

Voices by Joan Aiken
Julia had been told by people in the village that Harkin House was haunted. And ever since moving in to the house for the summer, she'd been troubled by violent dreams. What had happened in the old house's turbulent past?

The Nightmare Man by Tessa Krailing
Alex first sees the man of his darkest dreams at Stackfield Pond. And soon afterwards he and his family move in to the old house near the pond — End House — and the nightmare man becomes more than just a dream.

A Wish at the Baby's Grave by Angela Bull
Desperate for some money, Cathy makes a wish for some at the baby's grave in the local cemetery. Straight afterwards, she finds a job at an old bakery. But there's something very strange about the bakery and the two Germans who work there. . .

The Bone-Dog by Susan Price
Susan can hardly believe her eyes when her uncle Bryan makes her a pet out of an old fox-fur, a bone and some drops of blood — and then brings it to life. It's wonderful to have a pet which follows her every command — until the bone-dog starts to obey even her unconscious thoughts. . .

All on a Winter's Day by Lisa Taylor
Lucy and Hugh wake up suddenly one wintry morning to find everything's changed — their mother's disappeared, the house is different, and there are two ghostly children and their evil-looking aunt in the house. What has happened?

The Old Man on a Horse by Robert Westall
Tobias couldn't understand what was happening. His parents and little sister had gone to Stonehenge with the hippies, and his father was arrested. Then his mother disappeared. But while sheltering with his sister in a barn, he finds a statue of an old man on a horse, and Tobias and Greta find themselves transported to the time of the Civil War. . .

Look out for these forthcoming titles in the HAUNTING series:
The Rain Ghost by Garry Kilworth
The Haunting of Sophy Bartholomew by Elizabeth Lindsay

HIPPO BOOKS FOR OLDER READERS

If you enjoy a really good read, look out for all the
Hippo books that are available right now. You'll find
gripping adventure stories, romance novels, spooky
ghost stories and all sorts of fun fiction to keep you
glued to your book!

HAUNTINGS: Ghost Abbey by Robert Westall £1.95
The Little Vampire in Love
by Angela Sommer-Bodenberg £1.25
Snookered by Michael Hardcastle £1.50
Palace Hill by Peter Corey £1.95
Black Belt by Nicholas Walker £1.75
**STEPSISTERS 1: The War Between the
Sisters** by Tina Oaks £1.75
THE MALL 1: Setting Up Shop
by Carolyn Sloan £1.75
Conrad's War by Andrew Davies £1.75
Cassie Bowen Takes Witch Lessons by Anna
Grossnickle Hines £1.75
Tales for the Midnight Hour by J B Stamper £1.75
Creeps by Tim Schock £1.50

You'll find these and many more fun Hippo books at
your local bookshop, or you can order them direct. Just
send off to *Customer Services, Hippo Books, Westfield
Road, Southam, Leamington Spa, Warwickshire CV33
OJH*, not forgetting to enclose a cheque or postal order
for the price of the book(s) plus 30p per book for postage
and packing.

CAN'T GET THE GIRL

CAN'T GET THE GIRL

Adapted from
Phil Redmond's Hollyoaks
by
Karen Dolby

A CHANNEL FOUR BOOK

■ sapling

The publishers would like to thank Phil Redmond for
his help and advice in producing this book.

First published in Great Britain in 1996 by Sapling,
an imprint of Boxtree Limited, Broadwall House,
21 Broadwall, London SE1 9PL

ISBN 0 7522 0150 6

10 9 8 7 6 5 4 3 2 1

A CIP catalogue entry for this book is available from
the British Library

Typeset by SX Composing DTP, Rayleigh, Essex
Printed in Great Britain by
Cox & Wyman Ltd, Reading, Berks

Chapter 1

It was eight-twenty on a Monday morning. Tony Hutchinson was riding his Honda to his girlfriend, Julie's house. He was worried. Ever since Kurt's party things had not been the same between them. Tony suspected that she had been avoiding him. He hoped to meet her this morning as she walked to school, to clear up any misunderstanding. Had Tony noticed Julie appear outside her house and disappear quickly back indoors when she spotted his familiar figure arriving, all his worst fears would have been confirmed. As it was, he pulled up and hurried anxiously to her front door. Five minutes later Tony checked his watch. If he wasn't careful he would be late for work. He decided to ring the doorbell one more time. Julie must have left for school unusually early for him to have missed her.

Then he started to wonder whether she had meant to miss him. He began to feel uncomfortable, as if he was being watched. He pulled on his helmet and, looking thoroughly fed up, rode

1

miserably on his way to the college canteen and work.

Julie peered cautiously around her bedroom curtain and watched his motorbike until it disappeared from sight. She looked pale and strained. She was not very proud of what she'd done. She really liked Tony and he deserved to be treated better than this – or at least to have an explanation. Avoiding him and hiding was not the answer but the trouble was that the whole situation was proving too much for her. Everywhere they went they seemed to bump into Ollie, in the pub, at school and even Tony's best friend, Kurt, was Ollie's brother. There was no avoiding him and Ollie just could not accept that she no longer wanted to go out with him and was now seeing Tony. Julie could not bear any more of his accusing stares, malicious jibes or threats of a fight. Sighing, Julie picked up her school bag. She would have to run now and even then she would just have to hope that no teachers were around to catch her slipping into class late.

As the last few pupils hurried to their classrooms Ollie still hovered about in the corridor waiting in vain to catch Julie. 'Where *is* she?' he thought, impatiently. A member of staff, seeing Ollie loitering, pointedly tapped his watch.

'Yeah, yeah, I'm going,' Ollie muttered as he trudged reluctantly away to his first lesson.

Luck was not on Julie's side. She was about to hurry inside the main building when she heard her name called. Her shoulders dropped as she turned to try to explain why she was late to one of her teachers. Tony did not fare any better. He was still pondering the problem of what had gone wrong with Julie as he chained and padlocked his bike to the bins next to the college canteen where he worked, a necessary precaution against student pranks. His thoughts were soon interrupted when someone coughed loudly behind him. It was the canteen manager. Tony was late.

Dawn was also having a bad start to her day. She and Terry, her mother's boyfriend, were arguing again. Anyone watching Dawn's house would have seen the front door open and slam shut and heard angry voices. Terry was trying to stop Dawn from leaving. Finally, carrying her bag and coat Dawn struggled free. Terry wanted her to stay and finish the argument. Dawn was in no mood to do so and as Terry pulled her back she swung around and whacked him with her bag. Terry let go and, looking very annoyed, he watched Dawn storm off down the path.

She walked quickly away breathing deeply, trying to regain her composure and temper. Her hands were shaking and her knuckles were white where she gripped the shoulder strap of her bag. She gingerly touched her left eye, testing how sore it was. She hoped she was not going to have a black eye. The curious glances from the other people waiting at the bus stop prompted Dawn to check it surreptitiously in her compact mirror. It was red and showing signs of swelling. 'Damn, Terry,' Dawn swore to herself. That was all she needed. How on earth was she to explain it away? What would the customers think in the design shop where she worked?

The only problem with Kurt's morning was that the alarm had begun its insistent beeping and he had to get up. He was going to see the works manager on a building site to ask about a job. He had to do something to help him put together the money he needed to rebuild his Ford Consul which Ollie had 'borrowed' and trashed. Kurt groaned as the blind shot up and the room flooded with light. Jambo, who seemed incapable of staying in his own home, grinned as Kurt pulled a pillow over his eyes before slowly getting up and staggering unsteadily to the door. There was also another occupant of the bedroom. Margaret, the life-size model cow Jambo had borrowed as his 'date' for Kurt's party. It was now draped with Jambo's clothes, with a hat on its head and Kurt's acoustic guitar dangling from its neck. When Kurt returned ten minutes later, he looked more awake and normal. He was carrying two mugs of coffee and nodded towards the notice on Margaret's side.

'*Get rid of this*!' Jambo read. 'Your mother's got no charity,' he said.

'She always said I couldn't bring girls up here,' Kurt grinned. 'So when is it going?'

'Where am I supposed to put it?' Jambo asked.

'You should have thought of that before you nicked it!' Kurt said.

'Liberated . . .' Jambo corrected. Kurt sipped his coffee and waited for Jambo to come up with a solution. His mother had given him a lot of flack over the cow.

'It's handy for your guitar and clothes – a "clothes cow"?' Kurt still waited.

'Well I can't take it on the bus can I?' Jambo pleaded. 'What about your garage.' Kurt sighed. At least it was a start. 'O.K. – I'll help you shift it tonight,' said Jambo, just about to exit through the window.

'Wrong!' said Kurt pulling him back.

'Would now be convenient?' Jambo corrected himself.

'Now is very good.'

'I'll get her neck – you get the udder end,' Jambo grinned as Kurt groaned and the two began to manoeuvre the cow downstairs.

Chapter 2

Later that morning, Ollie managed to get out of a lesson a few minutes early. He quickly made his way to the science lab and watched the stream of pupils leaving when the changeover bell sounded. He peered through the window in the door and saw Julie slowly gathering her books. Ollie swallowed nervously, unsure whether this was such a good idea. When Julie came out Ollie had his back to the door. She took one look at Ollie and, without saying a word, she started to hurry away in the opposite direction. Ollie turned and seeing her almost running instinctively rushed after her and grabbed her bag to stop her. Julie swung round, looking pale.

'I don't want to talk to you,' she snapped. Why couldn't he just leave her alone? This was not doing anyone any good at all. Ollie stared back at her not saying anything. Then, 'I'm sorry about Kurt's party, I know I was out of order.' He paused. 'But I want to know why you dumped me.'

'Oh, please Ollie . . . not again,' Julie sighed

with frustration. 'I just don't want to go out with you anymore.'

'Why?' Ollie couldn't understand because he did not want to understand. He knew he was behaving like an idiot and making everything worse. He should just leave Julie alone. But he couldn't.

'You know why,' Julie sighed. Ollie stared back stubbornly. 'Because of all this.'

'All this what?'

'This!' Julie almost yelled with exasperation. 'This hassle!'

'I never gave you any hassle until Tony came along.'

Julie bit her lip. This was not doing any good at all. She turned to go. 'I'm going to be late.'

'I want to talk about it,' Ollie said sulkily.

'Not now,' Julie began. She was saved by the appearance of one of the teachers. They should both have been at their next class. Julie hurried to her classroom. She had gained a temporary reprieve but not for long. At lunchtime Julie and Ollie were both with their own friends outside school. They noticed one another at the same moment and stared warily at each other before Julie began to walk away.

This was the trigger that Ollie needed. He shouted angrily to her to stop. 'I want to talk to you!' But Julie did not stop. Ollie began to run after her. Hearing him chasing her, Julie also began to run. To the surprised stares of their friends, Julie closely followed by Ollie, disappeared around the corner of the school building. Running as fast as she could, Julie dashed inside and raced along a corridor with Ollie still in hot pursuit. She ran up a flight of stairs to the top floor along a corridor and then down another stairwell almost slipping in her hurry. As she reached the bottom step Ollie appeared at the top. Julie ran on, more than a little breathless now. She started along the corridor towards the gym and realized too late that it was a dead end. She stopped, trying to get her breath and decide which way to go. She looked back up the corridor. There was no sign of Ollie and there was a good chance that he had not seen which way she went. Ollie was feeling irritated but he could not bring himself to give up the chase. He asked a boy if he had seen Julie and quickly set off towards the gym. As soon as Julie saw him come through the doors at the far end she turned, saw the exterior fire doors and, thinking only of escape, charged through and away. Ollie caught a glimpse and sped after her.

Once outside there was nowhere else to go but a low-level teaching block straight ahead. Julie dashed inside into a locker room. Ollie did not see where she went but he also reasoned that there was nowhere else and followed her in. Julie tried to find somewhere to hide but quickly realized she had run into another dead end. She opened the door and saw Ollie. Quietly she reclosed the door and tried to creep away. As she did, she backed into one of the open

metal locker doors. Clang! It crashed back noisily. She froze knowing there was no chance that
Ollie had not heard. The door slowly opened.
Silently Julie tiptoed to the end of the row of
lockers and then round into the next aisle. She
flattened herself back against one of the lockers, closed her eyes and hoped.

It was useless. Ollie walked into the room. He
was still annoyed at having to chase her around
the school. He tried calling her name but there
was no reply. Feeling more and more tense Julie
listened to his footsteps coming closer, walking
up to the end of the row. Soon he would reach
her aisle. She was desperate to get away. She
could not bear to be caught now. Frantically
Julie looked for some escape, but there was
nowhere. She summoned up what strength and
energy she had left and waited. Just as Ollie
appeared around the end of the aisle, Julie
rushed at him, catching him by surprise . . . and
off-balance. He crashed back against the wall
but managed to grab hold of her jacket. As a
result, when Julie tried to run away she was
caught and banged against the lockers. One of
the open doors swung back and bashed her face,
cutting her mouth. The only good thing was
that as she bounced off the lockers, she shoved
Ollie, who stumbled and fell, giving Julie time
to get away. She left Ollie rubbing his side and,
far from looking like the crazed tormentor that
Julie had visualized, he looked close to tears.

Meanwhile, Tony had been preparing for lunch hour at the college . . . and worrying about Julie. He was restocking a sandwich machine when he met Natasha. She quickly sensed his mood.

'You look as bad as I feel,' she commiserated.

Tony smiled in acknowledgement. 'Aren't you going down to the canteen for lunch?'

'I can't stand yet another rerun of "The Adventures of Kurt and Louise",' Natasha grimaced.

'Still milking it, is she?'

'Double cream,' Natasha smiled ironically. Louise and Kurt had been her idea after all, though it somehow did not seem quite such a good joke now. 'At least we cheered her up.'

'Gave her back her self esteem and "empowerment".'

'Sounds like a Kurt Benson line.'

Tony nodded. 'All we need now is for someone to sort out our lives. So what's up with you?'

'I'll be O.K. when Louise calms down,' Natasha shrugged. 'What's up with you – Julie trouble? Is she cooling off?'

'I suppose so – how did you know?' Tony looked thoroughly miserable.

'I am one of the enemy remember?' Natasha quipped referring to Kurt and a previous conversation. 'Is she under pressure from Ollie? He wasn't exactly thrilled that you took his girl-friend away . . .'

'I didn't. Julie dumped him,' Tony was defensive.

'That's not the way Ollie sees it. Look how he acted at Kurt's party. And they *are* at the same school.'

Suddenly it all began to make more sense to Tony. He looked at his watch and seemed to reach a decision. 'Thanks Nat. I owe you one,' Tony reached into the machine before locking it and tossed Natasha a pack of sandwiches. To her surprise Tony then raced away down the corridor going in the opposite direction from the canteen.

He arrived at Julie's school to find her group of friends animatedly discussing what had just happened. Tony rode off to try to find Julie – and Ollie.

He soon saw Julie hurrying away from the teaching block, holding a tissue to her mouth. Julie had no desire to see anyone, but when Tony called her name, whether through fatigue or fatalism she sighed and stopped, waiting for him to catch up with her.

'What's happened?' Tony was immediately anxious.

Before Julie could answer Ollie appeared at the door of the teaching block already calling after her. He stopped when he saw Tony. Tony looked at Ollie, back at Julie's cut lip and jumped to the obvious conclusion. Furious, he charted towards Ollie who turned and fled. Julie was left alone watching the two chasing away. She looked frustrated, angry and hurt.

Ollie came thundering around the side of a building on to the playing field. Tony was in hot pursuit and closing the gap. He had been an excellent rugby player at school and had obviously lost none of his old skills. He tackled Ollie, diving for his ankles and bringing him down cleanly. Ollie struggled to get free but Tony was on top of him trying to pin him down. Tony slapped Ollie across the head and tried to get hold of his hair to keep him still. Ollie still struggled like crazy.

'Did you do that to her?' Tony yelled

'No!!!'

Tony was about to slap Ollie again when he realized that the resistance had gone out of his body. To his shocked surprise he saw that Ollie was sobbing. This made Tony sit back, allowing Ollie to roll on to his side still crying. Tony was completely taken aback. This was not at all what he had expected. He sat on the ground next to Ollie fighting to get his breath back. Slowly Ollie pulled himself together and also sat up, wiping his eyes and face with his sleeve.

Tony was unable to stop himself feeling concerned. 'Are you all right?' he asked.

'What do you care?' Ollie snapped.

This was too much for Tony. He kicked out at Ollie. 'So,' he sounded tough again. 'Did you do that to her?'

'It was an accident,' Ollie sounded genuinely sorry. 'I didn't mean to hurt her. She rushed at

12

me. I grabbed her and she fell against the lockers. A door caught her.' Ollie trailed off, staring at the ground, lost in his own thoughts.

He suddenly looked very young and by contrast Tony felt much older and more mature. He was no longer angry and he felt sorry for Ollie, knowing that with Julie definitely cooling towards him he was about to go through similar misery.

'Horrible isn't it?' Tony spoke kindly. 'Jealousy, rejection.'

Ollie was surprised. He did not want anyone's pity and especially not his rival's. But something in Tony's voice made him look up. He realized that Tony actually meant it, he was being genuinely sympathetic.

'I just lost it. I couldn't handle my temper,' Ollie had to make one dig. 'Like you couldn't with me.'

Tony took the point and stood up, offering his hand to help Ollie stand.

'I remember when the only thing we used to fight about was who would be next on Streetfight II,' Tony grinned.

'Usually Kurt,' Ollie and Tony grinned. Ollie winced in horror as a ghastly thought occurred to him. 'You . . . won't tell Kurt about this will you?'

'About upsetting Julie?'

Ollie looked embarrassed. He pointed to the ground and then to his eyes.

'No,' Tony shook his head. 'Unless you give

me grief in the future, of course.'

Ollie grinned. 'It is hard. I really fancied her – I still do.'

Tony looked understanding, more out of consideration of his own position. 'What are you going to do?' he asked.

Ollie shrugged. 'Dunno – try a ouija board like Louise – or just try and "get over it" I suppose.' With that the school bell rang indicating the end of the lunch break. Tony suddenly realized what he had done. Knowing he was probably in deep trouble, he rushed off to his motorbike to head back to the canteen as quickly as possible.

He reached college in record time. Still muttering to himself, he fumbled with the locking chain on his bike and, not daring to think, he rushed towards the canteen entrance – to find the manager standing in the doorway. To say he looked displeased would be an understatement. Tony looked at the sky for inspiration as he felt his whole world collapsing about him.

Chapter 3

Kurt was working at his computer with his guitar on his lap. He was also talking on the phone to Jambo. 'I'm simply speaking on behalf of one cow about another,' he quipped. 'How did she put it – "Just get the flaming thing moved!" She doesn't want it in the garage. Tonight . . .? Cool!'

Kurt hung up and looked thoughtful as he always did when working on his song 'Can't Get the Girl'. He frowned as he thought about Natasha, especially when he repeated the last three lines, *'Can't get the girl . . . Late at night – time running out . . . Had all day – didn't know what to say . . .'* He shook his head. It said the right things but the verse was not working. Perhaps he should bin the whole thing.

He had been in a buoyant mood all day. His interview at the building site had gone well. He was to start the next day for a couple of weeks' work. On the way back he had then had a very satisfactory run in with the police who had spotted his infamous 'Flying Virgin' helmet and tried to chase him round a roundabout and intercept him. Kurt had given them the slip by unexpectedly pulling on to the roundabout itself and then heading off along the exit that the police car had just that instant passed. He turned back to his lyrics as Ollie came in.

'Tony's here,' Ollie said. Kurt thought he had misheard. Ollie would not even speak Tony's name of late. 'Tony,' Ollie repeated casually.

'As in Tony who dated your girlfriend?'

'Yeah.'

Puzzled, Kurt put down his guitar and followed Ollie downstairs. Tony was Ollie's mortal enemy. He was even more surprised when he reached the kitchen. Tony looked anxious and was nervously twisting a fork around but there did not appear to be any problem between him and Ollie who was nonchalantly making two mugs of coffee.

'I might have lost my job,' Tony said when he saw Kurt. 'I went missing at lunchtime when we had the new area manager in.'

Kurt was still watching Ollie, waiting for an eruption. He did not quite understand Tony's problem. 'And you knew this management guy was on site?' Tony nodded, looking down and irritable. 'Why go missing then?'

Tony sighed. He might as well explain otherwise Kurt would go on asking questions. 'I had to see Julie.'

Kurt glanced across at Ollie expecting a reaction. He was still confused. 'You went to see Julie when you should have been working?' he

16

looked at Tony as if he was mad. Tony was normally so sensible.

'I had to sort something out. I went to see her at school.' Kurt again looked across at Ollie but his only reaction was to hand Tony one of the mugs of coffee and smile in a friendly, sympathetic manner.

By now Kurt was completely perplexed. 'Where's mine?'

Ollie nodded towards the kettle. 'Still in a chemically uncombined state.' He grinned at Kurt and left. Kurt stared at Tony sipping his coffee, made by Ollie. After a moment he leant across the table, picked up the fork and stabbed Tony in the hand. This caused Tony to jump and spill his coffee.

'What!' he yelped. 'Are you mental?'

'I was just testing in case you were an alien who had taken over Tony's body – or in case I was in an episode of *The X Files*.' Now it was Tony's turn to look at Kurt as if he was off the planet. 'What's going on here Tone? Only a week ago you and buddy beast out there were trying to kill each other . . . That's it!' Kurt leapt up and examined his face in the mirror. 'I'm in *Quantum Leap*.' He was still not taking in the seriousness of Tony's predicament.

'Please – I've got a career-threatening situation here.'

Kurt at last recognised the tone of despair in Tony's voice and gave him his full attention. 'What did you tell this management suit?'

Tony sighed. He knew it was a pathetic excuse. 'My dad had an industrial accident at work.'

'Your dad's an accountant. What did he do – get a nasty paper cut?' seeing the misery on Tony's face, Kurt conceded that it sounded a reasonable excuse.

'Until he checks,' Tony sighed. 'At least Dad's away on an audit for two days.'

Kurt was thinking fast. 'We'll just have to make sure your dad gets in first,' he grinned. Tony looked alarmed. 'Do you have a number for this guy?' Tony shook his head too quickly. 'It only needs one phonecall,' Kurt concluded.

'You don't even sound like my dad!'

'How could your dad phone if he's in surgery getting a staple removed from his finger?' he laughed at Tony's puzzled face. 'But your mother isn't . . . Hi dude – Tony's maternal here. Outstanding behaviour letting the lad off to visit his dad in intensive care. Terrible case of VDU-itis.'

Tony looked horrified. 'You can't.'

'I can't, but I know who can.'

Dawn had gone straight to Natasha's home when she finished work, waiting for her outside the pub sign until she saw her getting out of a car at the end of her driving lesson. Natasha noticed Dawn's now blackened eye immediately. They went inside while Dawn explained what had happened.

Natasha was worried about her friend. 'Dawn, it really is getting worse – the situation at home. You should go to the police.' Natasha nodded towards her eye, 'And you have to do something about that.' She knew she was wasting her breath.

'I could have done it myself – against the door,' Dawn said. Natasha looked unconvinced.

There was a knock and Natasha's father, Greg walked in. He was worried about Natasha's younger sister, Sarah. She was back in her room moping and looking miserable. He wanted Natasha to try to cheer her up and get her interested in going out again. Greg left and Dawn looked curious.

'Sarah hasn't really been the same since she was in the car crash with Benson's brother, Ollie,' Natasha explained. Sarah was Julie's best friend and when Julie was still going out with Ollie they had both been with him when he and Sarah's boyfriend took Kurt's car joy riding – with disastrous results. 'Every so often she goes into a type of depression and stays in her room for days.'

'Does your dad know who else was involved in the car crash?' Dawn asked. Natasha shook her head. Dawn grinned. 'Bet he doesn't know who you would like to be involved with, either.'

'I would not,' Natasha protested. Dawn gave her a knowing 'get real' type of look. 'Anyway,' Natasha sighed. 'Especially not now that Louise has told the entire college how besotted he was with her.' Dawn guessed correctly that this was the real reason that Natasha had seemed so down since Kurt's party. She really did like Kurt Benson but there was absolutely no way that her pride would let her become involved with him.

Downstairs, Greg was collecting glasses from the river deck outside the pub in the lull between afternoon and evening trade. Julie arrived. Like everyone today, it seemed, she looked a bit down.

'Hello,' said Greg. 'What happened to your lip?'

Julie looked self-conscious, 'Hockey . . .'

'None of my business, I know.'

Julie smiled. She liked Mr Anderson. He wasn't like most people's parents.

'I've been there a few times,' he added sympathetically. 'Sarah's in. It looks as though you two will be a right pair of bookends tonight. Go on through . . .' Greg paused as a better idea occurred to him. It was just the excuse he needed to get Sarah to come out of her room. 'On second thoughts you wait here. I'll bring her down.'

Julie flopped down on a bench to wait in the early evening sunshine. No sooner had she done so than she saw Kurt walking towards the pub with Tony. Julie's only escape route was the pub and she raced inside. Once in, Julie hesitated at the access hatch to the bar and the door to the Andersens' flat beyond. With no one around, she did not like to go on through. She began to panic as she heard the guys' voices on their way inside. Beginning to feel this was becoming a habit, she looked for somewhere to hide and disappeared into the toilets.

'Why do you want to work on a building site?' Tony asked.

'I don't want to but I need to – to get the money to finish the car. I'll be well paid,' Kurt explained.

'It's a stupid idea. Like that ouija board – and look where that got you.'

Kurt accepted this but added, 'Which is why someone owes me now.' As he spoke Natasha, Dawn and Sarah walked into the bar from the back. 'And speaking of the Angels of Mercy . . .'

'What do you want, Benson?' Natasha asked, coolly. Sarah carried on outside to look for Julie.

'Would you believe – you!?' Kurt smiled.

Natasha looked surprised, Dawn suspicious but before she could question him Kurt asked, 'What happened to your eye?'

This threw Dawn completely. 'I er . . . walked into a door . . . I mean a roll of fabric, in the shop . . . on the racks . . . behind the door – that I nearly walked into . . .' Natasha nudged her to shut up. Kurt and Tony found this rather odd but were interrupted by Greg who noticed Kurt and walked over to ask if he would like another gig.

'Providing the deal's right – usual dressing-room riders, all the drink I can consume,' Kurt grinned, joking.

'The dressing room will be the same,' Greg pointed to the lavatories. 'And you can have all the drink you can get out of one bottle,' he smiled, broadly, 'of Seven Up . . . between you.'

Greg was needed in the restaurant and Natasha again asked what Kurt and Tony wanted. By now Tony had lost what little confidence he had in the idea in the first place. He wanted to forget the whole thing. 'It was a stupid idea. Let's go,' he said to Kurt.

This really intrigued Dawn and Natasha, a fact that was not lost on Kurt.

'Is trying to help your best friend a stupid idea?' he asked, playing their interest for all it was worth. 'Any more so than other people helping their best friend by doing an ouija board?' Dawn and Natasha looked at one another. 'Or any more stupid than landing an innocent bystander with said best friend?' Dawn and Natasha now looked a little guilty. This *did* involve them. Kurt carried on. 'Which said "best friend" could have been, severely and permanently, emotionally damaged if said "innocent bystander" had not been so sensitive, so caring, so aware of other people's feelings. Do I need to say more?'

'All right, Benson. What do you want us to do?'

Kurt grinned as he ushered them all to a booth to explain. Sarah popped into the pub, looked around for Julie and, not seeing her, went outside. She soon returned wondering where Julie had got to and t̶ the only place left to look.

Kurt finished explaining To̶n̶y̶ with the canteen manager and it w̶ that Dawn would be the best one out o̶f girls to make the phone call. She began en̶t̶e̶r̶ing the number on her mobile phone. 'I must be mad,' she muttered. Natasha was looking apprehensive and Tony openly anxious. The phone rang a couple of times and then Dawn began speaking in a more mature, older-sounding voice than usual.

'Mr Stanstead, so glad to have caught you,' she began. 'It's Mrs . . .' she looked panicky as she realized she did not have a clue what Tony's surname was. She pretended to cough looking encouragingly at Tony who just looked blank.

Fortunately Kurt guessed the problem, 'Hutchinson.'

'Helen,' Tony snapped awake, at last.

Dawn stopped coughing. 'So sorry. It's Helen Hutchinson here . . . Ye-es, Anthony's mother. I wanted to phone and thank you for being so understanding at lunchtime. Poor Anthony was in such a state about his father . . . Just dashed off without thinking, bless him . . .'

Tony was cringing – this was never going to work. Kurt was smirking, trying not to laugh and Natasha was rolling her eyes. In the background Jambo's head appeared at one of the other windows looking for his mates.

'What was that? Oh dear . . .' Dawn looked in

. . . . others for help which was the
. . . . ment that Jambo chose for his entrance, diving through the open window over their table,
crashing on to Dawn's lap. In her normal voice,
she yelled automatically, 'Get off you idiot!'
Kurt grabbed Jambo and, gagging him before
he could say anything, he dragged him off. Not
for the first time that day, Tony looked as
though his whole world was about to collapse.
Natasha thought it was all over but Dawn
recovered quickly.

'No . . . no . . . just the animal,' she scowled
meaningfully at Jambo. 'He's a bit of a handful
but we love him. What was I saying . . . Oh yes .
. . what happened? Well we're not quite sure,'
she pulled a face and shrugged. Tony looked as
if he couldn't take much more. Kurt smiled
encouragingly but no one offered any help.
Dawn thought hard. 'The doctors want to keep
him in overnight for tests and . . .' in a flash of
inspiration Dawn concluded, 'I'm afraid I must
go, there's the taxi to take me to the hospital. I
must fly. Thank you again for not being too
hard on Anthony . . . Yes . . . I'll tell him.
Goodbye.' With a long sigh, Dawn hung up and
fell back against her seat.

'Awesome!' said Kurt, impressed.

'I'm finished,' Tony groaned.

'He said to tell you not to worry – he under-
stands,' Dawn laughed. Tony pinched himself
to make sure he was not dreaming and laughed,
too.

24

'Who gave you the eye?' Jambo looked quizzically at Dawn, seeing her bruise for the first time. Dawn pulled a face. She did not want to talk about it. But Jambo noticed her mood drop several degrees. He liked Dawn and felt suddenly protective. 'If you want anyone seeing to, let me know.' Jambo looked uncharacteristically serious. He held Dawn's surprised stare for a moment. There was a flicker of recognition – of a shared hurt and sensitivity. 'I mean it,' Jambo paused and then switched back into his normal persona. 'So – what was that all about?'

'Dawn just saved Tony's job,' Kurt smiled.

'And paid off the Louise favour,' Natasha added.

Kurt nodded, accepting the deal. 'So Tone – not a care in the world now,' Kurt followed Tony's eyeline across the bar, to where Sarah and Julie had just walked in. 'Well . . . almost.'

Tony took a deep breath and went across to Julie. Diplomatically, Sarah left to wait outside. At first, Tony and Julie just looked awkwardly at one another. Finally Tony spoke. 'I'm sorry about earlier but,' he paused, fishing for the right words, 'I wanted to come and see you to ask – if you were avoiding me, because Ollie was . . .'

'Giving me a hard time?' Julie finished for him. Tony nodded. 'He was. And I was in when you called this morning. Then I was in trouble for being late, then there was Ollie following me, then chasing me, then my lip.' Julie didn't need to say more.

'So you can do without it all?' Tony asked sadly. From Julie's silence, the answer was obvious. 'I suppose there's no chance of trying again, now Ollie's accepted everything?'

'I'm only fifteen – I'm too young for all this hassle,' Julie leant across and kissed his cheek quickly. She was sorry because Tony was nice. They'd had fun and maybe without the extra problems with Ollie things could have been different. As it was, the only answer seemed to be to split up. Julie turned quickly and hurried out. Tony looked crestfallen and close to tears as he also headed for the door.

Kurt and Natasha who had been watching out of genuine concern for Tony, were about to follow when Greg and Sarah rushed in.

'You lot know anything about a cow outside?' called Greg. Everyone looked at Jambo who took a last gulp of his drink and dived back out through the window.

Chapter 4

On Saturday, Kurt was up early for his job on the building site and Jambo's cow, Margaret, was out on her travels once more. This time at the garden centre. Jambo was pushing the cow on a trolley and had covered her with a huge dust sheet so that it was impossible to tell exactly what was on the trolley. Even so, Jambo gave constant furtive looks over his shoulder to make sure the coast was clear as he pushed the trolley across the yard towards where the garden-centre truck was parked. He stopped several times to adjust the dust sheet and make sure that Margaret was completely hidden. Jambo manoeuvred the cow on to a loading-bay platform and reversed the truck back towards her. That done he began to push Margaret along an improvised ramp between the platform and the back of the truck. Halfway across she got stuck. Her dust sheet slipped and as Jambo sprang forward to swish it back in place, he froze.

'James? What is going on here?' It was the unmistakable voice of Mr Gardner, the owner of the garden centre. Jambo's face went through contortions of anguish as he turned towards him. Mr Gardner stood considering Margaret and waiting for an answer.

Without pause for breath or thought, Jambo's brain shifted up a gear. Instead of trying to pull the sheet back over the cow he carefully unfolded it. 'Well, Mr Gardner, what do you think?' he asked seriously. Mr Gardner looked confused. Jambo stood back as if to admire Margaret. 'I've arranged for you to have her on loan for a couple of weeks.' Mr Gardner now looked completely puzzled. Jambo explained. 'The summer plant promotion. What is the ideal summer image? Green fields, summer flowers, butterflies and . . . cows!'

Unfortunately for Jambo, Mr Gardner was not taken in. 'This is a garden centre. We sell plants. Where did you get it? I want the truth now.'

Jambo knew when to admit defeat. 'Do you know Buddleworth Farm?'

Mr Gardner stepped forward to examine Margaret more closely. 'Is this one of Bill Sorenson's?' he asked. Jambo's heart and face sank as Mr Gardner continued. 'He used to have six of these on the roof of his dairy shed.'

'This was in the corner of the field by Dead Man's Pond,' Jambo explained.

'Where no doubt it was quite happy until you came along,' Mr Gardner was interrupted by a request over the tannoy system for him to come

28

to the telephone. 'You had better wait here, James. You and I need a serious chat.'

Jambo patted Margaret and sat down next to her to wait. Ten minutes later Jambo was still waiting. He watched a woman making her way back to her car with a trolley laden with pots, and bedding plants. She seemed to be struggling with the trolley and Jambo quickly realized that she was not going to make it to the car. Jambo dashed over – just in time to catch one of the trays of bedding plants as it began to slide. The woman looked relieved and cheered by Jambo's smile. He then handed her the tray and pushed the trolley towards her car. Mr Gardner arrived as all this was going on. He watched Jambo cheerily chatting and helping to load the car and, smiling to himself, went back inside the garden centre. He'd decided to let Jambo stew a little.

Half an hour later, Jambo was still awaiting Mr Gardner and was now talking to a man with a trolley full of heathers to which Jambo was adding a few more along with his advice. The man's two young children were having a lovely time climbing on Margaret and pretending to ride her. As the man made his way to the pay desk, Jambo sent the children happily scurrying after their father.

'Time to go, you two,' he said. 'Margaret has to go in to be milked.'

'That's not a real cow . . .' one said, looking at Jambo, uncertain if he was joking or not.

'Can we come and see her again?' the other asked.

Jambo was watching the children rejoin their father and so did not notice Mr Gardner standing behind him.

'So?' said Mr Gardner. 'Did they just gawp, or did they spend real money?'

'He spent money,' Jambo replied. 'Well, he did when the kids had stopped bothering him and were occupied elsewhere.'

Mr Gardner looked stern but a smile twitched at the corners of his mouth. 'Well, what have you got to say for yourself?'

'I'm very sorry it was . . . just a joke really. I am sorry. I don't want to lose my job, you know Mum finds it all a bit of a struggle on her own.'

Mr Gardner stopped him. Jambo's mother also worked at the garden centre, as a bookkeeper. 'I know all that, James. I'm very fond of your mother. She's the best bookkeeper I've ever had – which is why I let her talk me into giving you a job in the first place,' Mr Gardner grinned. 'And I admit you are a good worker. But . . . all that only goes so far and there's only one thing that's stopping me from kicking you out,' Mr Gardner could hardly stop himself chuckling at Jambo's worried, serious-looking face. 'And that's the fact that Bill Sorenson still owes me for thirty-five *leyllandi* I planted as a hedge next to his swimming pool and I always threatened to go and kidnap one of his damn cows.'

Jambo began to relax. 'Way to go Mr G.'

'But that was when I was young and foolish – like you and had no one to tell me better. So – get rid of her!'

Jambo began to enquire about whether he could borrow the truck to move her, which had been his original intention. That was going too far, however and Mr Gardner just pulled a 'don't push it' type of face and walked briskly back to his office.

'Now Margaret,' sighed Jambo. 'We really are on the horns of a dilemma.' How on earth was he going to shift the cow? At that moment, the solution to the problem arrived. Jambo grinned as Kurt rode into view.

Kurt had just finished his morning shift at the building site and had been riding along feeling very pleased with life and with a satisfyingly stuffed envelope holding his week's wages safely stashed in his jacket pocket. As always when riding his motorbike, he kept a sixth sense on the alert for the police and not unusually saw a police car – parked very unusually outside Tony's house. Seeing Tony's father, Brian, looking worried as he ushered two policemen inside, Kurt hid his bike and strolled up to the house to find out what was going on. When he had found out, he immediately set off to find Jambo.

He roared to a halt next to Jambo, pulled off his helmet and began to explain what was going on.

'Tony's missing,' he began, dramatically. 'He didn't go home last night and didn't tell his parents he was staying out.'

Jambo shrugged. He didn't know what the problem was. He stayed out all the time.

'It's not like "Mr Dependable", though is it? The most outrageous thing he's ever done is not handed back his textbooks when he left school,' said Kurt. 'Anyway, the only place he stays over is mine – and we know he wasn't there.'

Jambo was still not convinced and more concerned about moving the cow.

'We should go and look for him,' Kurt was genuinely worried. 'Something could have happened to him.'

'*Could* have. But something *is* going to happen to me if I don't shift Margaret,' Jambo reasoned. 'We can do both – look for Tony and take Margaret for a spin.'

Kurt realized he was not going to get anywhere unless he helped Jambo. He sighed and walked towards Margaret. They lifted her so that her front legs were on one garden-centre trolley which Jambo, sitting on the back of Kurt's bike, had hold of and her back legs were on a second trolley. With this unlikely 'trailer', Kurt started up the bike and rode steadily away, hoping that for once he would not meet any police cars.

In a secluded corner of a city park near Riverbank sixth-form college, a figure slumped awkwardly on a bench. The figure was leaning to one side and appeared to be asleep. But if anyone had been watching they would have been alarmed to see him slowly topple from the bench on to the ground where he lay motionless. It was Tony.

Chapter 5

Kurt knew they could not go far with Margaret and made their first stop Jambo's, where they deposited the cow with the two trolleys and Jambo collected a bag containing his football gear. He then headed for his own home in case Tony had called there. He collected his spare helmet for Jambo and went back to Tony's house to hear the latest news. There was still no sign of him.

'I wonder if my mum is as upset as that when I stay at yours,' Jambo mused when they walked back out of the house.

'Yours isn't,' said Kurt. 'Mine is!'

Jambo grinned. 'It has to be aliens – they've abducted him.' Kurt looked unimpressed by this theory, but Jambo continued anyway. 'He's not with us, we know that; he's not with his family, they know that; he's not in the hospital, the cops know that; he's . . .'

'He's not with aliens,' Kurt interrupted him.

'That's a very parochial view you're taking. How do you know he's still on this planet?'

'I know someone who isn't.'

'C'mon,' coaxed Jambo. 'It's not that heavy. He's just stayed out all night. He'll turn up in his own good time.'

'It's not like him. You . . . me . . . yes. Tony? No. He hasn't even taken his bike.'

To stop Jambo answering, Kurt thrust the spare helmet at him and started the engine.

'He'll be fine,' said Jambo, checking his watch. 'We can scout out the city on the way.' Kurt looked puzzled, Jambo soon enlightened him. 'Dropping me off at the match. First round of the Cheshire Cup today,' Kurt noticed Jambo's football bag for the first time. 'Then you can get on with the manhunt. You should be good at it really . . .' Jambo grinned.

'And why is that?' Kurt knew he was feeding Jambo a line.

'The amount of time you've spent hunting Natasha!'

'I'd rather you prattled on about meeting aliens.'

'You've got more chance of that than dating . . .' Jambo could not say more. Kurt let the clutch go and the bike roared off, with Jambo struggling to hold on.

Natasha and Louise had arranged to meet Dawn for her lunchbreak from work. They walked away from the main shopping area to go down Souter Lane towards the river. All three were in a bright, chatty mood. After lunch at Old Orleans, they sat back drinking cappuccinos. Louise read the horoscope page of the magazine she had just bought.

'"'. . . a changed appearance often brings a change of life . . .",' she read. 'I was thinking of getting my hair done – bright red.'

'Is this about Scully from *X Files*?' asked Natasha.

'More Dr Crusher,' Louise said seriously.

'Is that one of the doctors at the health centre?' Dawn joked.

'*Star Trek* – actually,' said Louise.

'*Next Generation* – actually,' Dawn said.

Natasha tried to bring the talk back to a previous conversation. 'So – any suggestions?'

'Your hair is always gorgeous,' Louise sighed.

'I mean about Sarah,' Natasha looked concerned. 'What can we do to make her see there's a world beyond her bedroom.'

'Depression's a gloomy business – I've been there,' Louise shrugged. 'It's depressing.'

Dawn and Natasha exchanged looks.

'Why do you feel so responsible, Nat?' asked Dawn. 'It's not your fault her best friend was going out with the idiot brother of the guy you fancy.'

'I . . . do . . . not . . .' Natasha grinned. 'He fancies me. I've got to do something. Mum and Dad are getting really worried about her. She hardly ever goes out. She doesn't speak. Just stays in her room and plays Take That all night.'

'Perhaps you had better do something? said Dawn.

'But what? I can't take her under my wing and watch her all the time,' sighed Natasha.

'Why not? You did it to me,' said Louise.

'That was different. You had a broken heart.'

This gave Louise her cue for rambling on about the 'black abyss of heartache'. Dawn and Natasha struggled to keep straight faces while trying to encourage Louise to come to the point. Finally she did. '. . . It shatters your confidence. That's what's wrong with Sarah. She needs a good day out and a bit of fun – to see that there's more to be had out of life. A bit like the day I had with Joe at Alton Towers,' Louise looked wistful at the memory. But she had given Natasha an idea.

'That's a wicked idea. We could all go,' she said.

'Not me,' Louise shook her head. 'There would be too many painful memories for me.'

Dawn also liked the idea. 'Rubbish! You're well over that jerk, Joe, now. Check your magazine – it's bound to be in one of our horoscopes. I'll get another coffee before I have to get back.'

'Come on, Lou, we helped you,' Natasha added. 'You can help Sarah by coming to Alton Towers with us and making sure she has fun.'

In the park, Tony's comatose figure had attracted the attention of a small dog. Tony's contorted face made him look as if he was in pain. He groaned and suddenly woke with a

37

start. It took him a few moments to work out where he was lying and how he had come to be there. He then realized his leg felt warm and wet. He was puzzled until he saw the small mongrel still looking at him. He groaned and held his head. That was all he needed. Slowly he stood up, staggered a few steps and sat down again quickly on the bench. He looked very sad and reached into his pocket where there was a crumpled strip of four passport-booth photos – he looked at himself and Julie smiling happily. He hastily tucked the photos away and began walking towards the college.

Across town, Natasha and Dawn were getting very excited about their proposed day out at Alton Towers. Plans were well under way.

'We'll get Maddie to come in her car – so there will be the three of us, Maddie and Sarah,' decided Natasha.

'I think Sarah should bring someone her own age, one of her friends,' Louise said.

'She could take Julie,' Dawn suggested. 'Since she's not seeing Tony any more. But then we wouldn't fit in the car.'

'I could drop out,' said Louise, sounding martyrish.

'We could squeeze up,' Dawn said.

'We could ask other people,' Natasha spoke casually.

'Like someone you don't fancy but who fancies you?' Louise teased.

'His car should be ready soon,' Natasha said defensively.

Dawn was about to add something when her attention was taken by two new customers who had just arrived at the cafe. She froze when she recognized her mother and Terry, obviously looking for a table. Terry soon spotted the girls and grinned as he sauntered across with Angela.

'Darling, I'm so glad we ran into you. We were going to stop by the shop,' Angela began, 'I have to go over to the Millbrook Centre later. One of their people had to pull out of a seminar and they've asked me to stand in. I'll be away until tomorrow but Terry will be at home if you need anything.'

Dawn's heart sank. Terry, meanwhile, winked at Natasha and eyed her appreciatively.

'Hi girls,' he smiled oilily. 'Room for two more?'

Louise and Natasha squirmed. 'We were just going,' Dawn answered coldly.

'Don't rush, we can go inside,' Angela smiled. 'It's a bit chilly when you get to our age.'

'Speak for yourself,' said Terry grinning. 'There's plenty of life left in me.'

Angela kissed Dawn, said goodbye and turned to go inside. Terry went to follow but stopped close to Dawn.

'See you later,' he bent as if to kiss her.

'Don't!' Dawn snapped.

Terry smiled. It was hard to tell if he was

teasing or not. 'See you tonight then,' he said. 'Nice cosy meal together.'

Natasha shuddered. 'This means we're all back to your place then tonight?'

'I can't leave Cindy alone with him,' Dawn looked anxious.

'He's never actually done anything, though,' said Natasha.

'Yet . . .'

The girls began gathering their things ready to leave.

Kurt and Jambo were cruising slowly through the people in Eastgate Street looking for Tony. As there was no sign of him, Kurt turned the bike down towards the river and Souters Lane. When they reached the roundabout at the edge of the river, Jambo spotted the three girls. Kurt brought the bike up next to them.

'Before you tell me to disappear,' said Kurt, 'have you guys seen Tony around anywhere?'

They all shook their heads and Kurt was about to move off when Natasha, after hesitating for a moment, called him back. She chewed her lip, still not entirely sure if she should or should not ask. Kurt turned and sat waiting for her to speak.

'Is that car of yours fixed yet?'

'Almost – I still need a fuel pump and rear-light cluster to match . . .' Kurt wondered what she was leading up to. Louise and Dawn smirked at each other.

'Never mind the details. Have you been to Alton Towers? Because we're thinking of making up a group – next week?'

Kurt was not altogether sure if he was being invited along or not and was worried about getting another knockback. He hesitated. 'Next week? I . . . I've got a job to help pay . . .'

Jambo could not stand this and butted in to speak for Kurt. 'He means, we'll be there.'

'Who asked you?' said Dawn.

It was Jambo's turn to look gutted until Dawn started to laugh.

'Right, yeah,' Kurt slipped back into cool mode. 'So, exactly what did you have in mind?'

Before Natasha could answer, Jambo thrust his watch under Kurt's nose and reminded him of their mission. 'Tony? Cheshire Cup?' he put his helmet back on.

'Gotta go,' Kurt said to Natasha. 'That's a date then?'

Natasha nodded but to make sure Benson did not get too big-headed added, 'One of thirty in the month.'

Kurt pulled a face and gunned the bike away. Natasha turned to face Louise and Dawn.

'He fancies you, eh?' Louise grinned.

'One of us has to try and get it together . . . or not!' Natasha laughed.

Tony trudged slowly past the college. But as he approached the main door he read a notice announcing, 'Riverbank Video Road Race

41

Championship'. A couple of people went inside and Tony hesitated. He thought for a moment and then, realizing he had nothing else to do, followed the others into the building.

Having dropped Jambo at his football match, Kurt had a decision of his own to make. Should he call on Julie and ask her about Tony? They were no longer going out but Kurt had a good idea that Tony's disappearance had a lot to do with the break-up and it was just possible that she might have an idea where he was. The trouble with Tony, Kurt pondered, was that he took women and relationships too seriously. You wouldn't catch him moping over a woman. With that thought he banished the image of Natasha from his mind and headed for Julie's house.

However, Julie had not seen Tony since they split up on Monday evening. Kurt waved and headed back to his bike to take another cruise around, searching for him. Julie stared thoughtfully after Kurt. She was worried about Tony. Since they split she'd had what she had wanted – a hassle-free week but she had found herself missing Tony and looking out for him on her walk to school.

Later that afternoon, having failed to find any clue as to Tony's whereabouts, Kurt went home. He took a shower to remove the building dust from his hair and phoned Tony's parents on his mobile. Tony had still not turned up. Kurt spoke into the phone as he

42

walked back into his room, rubbing his hair with a towel. He flicked off the phone, picked up his guitar and sat down at the computer. He hit the mouse to kill the screen-saver and the lyrics to Natasha's song 'Can't Get the Girl' appeared. Kurt began to strum the lyrics.

'Every time I see her my mind goes blank
Every time I see her my heart skips a beat
Can't get the girl
Can't get the girl . . .'

'Neither can I,' said a voice close behind him. Kurt leapt out of his skin and felt like he was about to have a heart attack.

Kurt whirled round to see Tony sprawled face-down on his bed. He looked bewildered.

'Ollie let me in,' Tony explained. 'Got anything for a headache?'

'Where the hell have you been?' Kurt exclaimed.

'Thinking,' Tony mumbled into Kurt's pillow. Kurt looked surprised and then completely confused when Tony looked up and added, 'I also got through the preliminary heat of the Video Road Race Competition.'

'Tone, rewind. Play it from the top,' begged Kurt.

'Have you ever really thought about sexual chemistry?' Tony said. Kurt sat down. 'You can't see anything happening when you fancy

43

someone, you can't really feel it . . .'

'That depends on what you're feeling.'

'You sort of sense it – tiny little chemical changes. And you know when it's over too, because the chemical reactions are different. Tiny reactions, yet they have such a massive impact,' Tony carried on.

'I gather this is about you and Julie?'

Tony was still thinking out loud. 'I never got any indication that she didn't fancy me, no chemical reactions, she just didn't want the hassle. I think she felt guilty, that she still fancies me but doesn't know how to cope with it, so . . . she took the easy way out.'

Kurt replied pragmatically, expounding his theory of male and female relations. 'Tone – don't try to figure women out, you've plenty of time for that. Right now it's simple – they've got what you want, there's plenty of them about, if one doesn't come across another will – ditch her and move on.'

'Like you're doing with Natasha?' Tony was sarcastic.

'Hey – that's choice, not necessity,' Kurt spoke sharply knowing he had been caught out. But it was true, he reasoned to himself. He was waiting around for Natasha out of choice and he had always moved quickly on in the past. He picked up the phone and handed it to Tony. 'And I never stayed out all night and had my folks phone the cops about me.'

Tony looked shocked as he grabbed the

phone. 'What's that terrible smell?' Kurt asked, sniffing.

'I'll tell you later . . .' Tony said, dialling.

The window slid open and Jambo appeared. He grinned when he saw Tony, who moved out of the room with the phone to talk in private.

'I see the wanderer's returned,' he said, straining to read the computer screen which still displayed Kurt's lyrics. Kurt quickly switched it off. Jambo also sniffed. 'Smells like a dog's backside in here.'

Kurt looked around puzzled, trying to locate the source of the smell.

'Where's he been?' asked Jambo.

'Studying chemistry, although biology would do him more good,' said Kurt, obliquely.

Jambo looked puzzled but soon nodded in agreement as if he understood what Kurt was on about.

'How'd you get on?'

'Won two nil and – Jambo opened the scoring!'

'Which is exactly what Tony needs to be doing.'

'Playing football?'

Kurt pulled a 'very funny' face as Tony walked back into the room still apologizing to his dad. He finally said goodbye and hung up. There was an awkward silence with no one quite sure what to say.

It was finally Jambo who suddenly said to Tony, 'It's time to show your vulnerable side.

Does Julie know she's reduced you to a gibbering idiot?'

Tony looked embarrassed and shook his head.

'Well actually . . . I'm afraid she does,' said Kurt. Tony flopped down on to the bed in cringing disbelief. Kurt waved the phone at him. 'No one knew where you were. If you'd put your faith in technology no one would have been worried.'

Jambo carried on with his own train of thought, 'Women are all trainee mothers. They all want to mother hen us . . .' Jambo held open his arms as though the solution was obvious.

'You sound as bad as Kurt,' groaned Tony. 'What am I supposed to do – go round to Julie's and burst into tears?'

Kurt and Jambo looked at each other as if this were a possibility worth considering. After due thought they shook their heads.

'What then? A bunch of flowers, box of chocolates, write her a song?' Tony nodded towards the computer.

Kurt glared at him. 'It's up to you how you do it.'

'You just need to tell her how you feel but . . .' Jambo sniffed, 'I'd have a wash first.'

'It was some dog – it . . .' Tony waved his trouser leg.

'What!?' Kurt exclaimed. 'That's my bed you're lying on.'

Washed and changed a couple of hours later, Tony paced up and down along Julie's street. He was holding chocolates and flowers and feeling very unsure of himself. Finally he walked quickly towards the house, paused and carried on past. He looked at the flowers and the chocolates and decided it was too much. He looked swiftly around to make sure no one was watching and hid the flowers behind a neighbour's wall. Feeling very self-conscious he again checked there was no one about. He turned back towards Julie's house but again his confidence failed him. This time he looked at the box of chocolates, decided they were also a naff idea and hid those along with the flowers. He marched back towards the house and turned away. Taking a deep breath he spun slowly round and stared at the front door. He took another deep breath and strode purposefully along the garden path, up the steps and knocked loudly on the knocker. There was no answer. He waited a few moments and tried a second time. Still there was no reply. After all that, she was out. There was nothing for it but to retrieve his chocolates and flowers and leave. He turned to go but was stopped by someone calling his name. Tony's face brightened as he saw Julie hurrying towards him. She was carrying a bunch of flowers and a box of chocolates. She began to run and without saying anything, she threw her arms around him and kissed him.

'I'm sorry,' she muttered.

Tony was delighted but puzzled. 'What for?'

'For being stupid,' Julie kissed Tony again. 'Did you really stay out all night thinking about me – us?'

Tony blushed faintly and looked embarrassed. Julie handed him the flowers and chocolates. It was now her turn to look embarrassed. 'I know it's a bit silly but . . . I saw it in *Neighbours*,' she shrugged.

Tony grinned and reached over the wall to retrieve his presents for Julie. 'It's really nice. I wanted to say sorry, too.'

They laughed and hugged one another again. 'At least none of the others can see us making fools of ourselves,' Tony smiled.

How wrong he was. From the street they heard: 'Smile for the camera!'

The camera flashed and behind it stood Kurt with Jambo leaning on his shoulder. They grinned inanely at the happy but rather shocked couple and generally looked very pleased with themselves.

Chapter 6

It was Sunday, just over a week later and the day finally agreed upon for the outing to Alton Towers. Kurt was up early working in the garage on the prop shaft of his car. Ollie came in carrying tea and toast. Kurt did not seem unduly surprised at this act of uncharacteristic brotherly kindness. Instead he asked Ollie why he had not also brought the radio from the kitchen.

'I can't carry everything,' Ollie snapped. 'I've paid off my debt to you, so why can't I come to Alton Towers?' – the real reason for the breakfast tray.

'Because Tony's back with Julie – he'll be taking her and he won't want you around,' Kurt explained.

'In case she realizes she still fancies me more than him and it was a mistake finishing with me,' Ollie grinned and obviously did not mean this seriously any more.

'Dream on Ol, dream on,' said Kurt. 'Anyway people who trash other people's cars have to learn respect. When you have, maybe then I'll let you come on the picnics with the grown-ups.'

'I think the real reason you don't want me to go is because I might tell Natasha what you're really like – smelly feet, secret Beach Boys fan and fighting a losing battle with spots,' Ollie wisely made his way to the door while speaking and shut it behind him in the nick of time, just avoiding a block of wood which Kurt hurled after him.

Kurt was smiling. He was in a good mood, looking forward to his day out and spending some time with Natasha.

Natasha meanwhile was still in bed, listening to Louise rambling on the telephone about why it would be so difficult for her to go to Alton Towers as it held so many painful memories for her.

'I quite understand, Louise. We couldn't possibly expect you to come with us,' Natasha opened a magazine and began reading as Louise rattled on again. A little later, with Louise still talking, Natasha began to get dressed. '. . . If the Haunted House had been where I'd kissed Joe for the first time,' interrupted Natasha, 'then I'd have great memories of it too . . . No, not if I'd kissed Joe, I mean if I was you. I don't really know what you saw in him in the first place.' As soon as she had spoken, Natasha wished she could take back her words. Louise was now going to go on even longer and take even longer to pacify. Sure enough, after discarding several possible outfits and changing completely once,

Natasha reached the make-up stage and still Louise was talking. 'We're hardly deserting you, Louise. I sympathize with you not wanting to come with us but to accuse us of disloyalty is a bit much . . . Well, I'm sorry if I've upset you.' Natasha looked to the heavens for inspiration and bit her lip. She knew that Louise would have to be pacified once more.

Jambo's morning had got off to a great start. He nipped into the newsagent to buy the latest copy of *Viz* and flicked through in eager anticipation. To his surprise, he found what he was looking for and punched the air with delight startling an old lady who happened to be walking by.

Jambo grinned at her and said, 'Salt flavoured vinegar.'

Not having a clue what he was talking about and assuming everyone his age was on drugs, she hurried away, casting anxious looks over her shoulder to make sure he was not following. Jambo didn't seem to notice.

When Tony arrived at the garden centre to meet Jambo he was intrigued to see him standing with an older woman. They were both laughing as they read something in a magazine. The woman quickly hugged Jambo who then walked away over to Tony.

'Who was that?' asked Tony curiously.

'Just some woman who thinks she owns me. Take a look at that then,' Jambo thrust the

51

copy of *Viz* at Tony and pointed at the appropriate passage.

'Jambo you're a genius,' said Tony admiringly. 'Weird, but a genius.'

Together they went to call for Kurt who had finished working on his car and was now admiring himself in the mirror. He was dressed in jeans, a white T-shirt and his black leather jacket. He adjusted his hair, passed himself fit for the world and more particularly for Natasha to see, stashed a photo wallet into his pocket and went downstairs to wait for Jambo and Tony.

Bazz, who along with Maddie was providing the transport, drew up outside Kurt's house. Kurt was puzzled to watch him driving backwards and forwards in the drive. Bazz did not notice Kurt as he concentrated on tuning his mobile radio scanner – he was picking up a signal that kept switching to another frequency and he was shifting the van to find the best position to receive the strongest signal. By now, Tony and Jambo had arrived. Kurt shrugged in answer to Tony's questioning look about the van driver's eccentricity. Kurt tried calling to Bazz and finally banged on the side of the van.

Bazz opened the door and Kurt, Tony and Jambo peered inside. Around the van's cab were speakers linked to a CD player and radio, tubes of small disco lights and an early-warning device for radar speed traps. Bazz's pride and joy was the mobile scanner plugged into the cigarette lighter. He looked conspiratorial and spoke in hushed tones. 'There's a guy called Whistle Blower who knows things. I don't know who he is but for weeks he's been putting out stuff about a big government cover up. Big stuff. Today's the day something's gonna happen.'

'Yeah,' said Kurt, sarcastically. 'Like today's the day we go to Alton Towers and we're meeting the others in fifteen minutes. So let's go.'

They climbed into the van and grinning, Kurt handed Tony the photo wallet. Inside was the photograph of Julie and Tony with the chocolates and flowers. Bazz set off to drive to the Dog in the Pond where they were all meeting. To Kurt's annoyance, Bazz was still fiddling with the radio scanner and looking increasingly impressed and intrigued with the information coming through.

'This is Whistle Blower, the voice of truth, the man in the know, your direct line into GCHQ. I've got to keep ducking and diving so you'll have to keep surfing to find me, because the thought police are searching since I tapped into the big one. The mega frequency for military use only and prohibited to unclassified personnel. I heard that the object is now passing over the southern Sahara Desert, trajectory stable and armed forces alerted.' The voice faded and Bazz quickly tried retuning, utterly convinced that the broadcaster was genuine.

'It's a wind-up,' said Kurt, equally convinced in his scepticism.

Dawn, along with her sister and brother, Cindy and Max, and Julie had arrived at Natasha's. Sarah was looking anxious, worrying about whether she should wear jeans or a skirt.

'Relax!' Natasha told her firmly, acting the big sister. 'We're going to have a wicked time – just wear what you'll be comfortable in – jeans will be fine. But hurry up – and make sure they're your own.'

They all went downstairs and sat at the tables on the pub decking where Maddie was already sitting to wait for the boys to arrive. Before long the pub door opened and Louise appeared.

'Changed your mind?' asked Natasha.

'I couldn't possibly, I just came to see you all off,' Louise sighed. Dawn and Natasha exchanged knowing looks. It would not be much of a gamble to bet that Louise ended up going with them. 'I expect I'll find something to do, but Sunday is the loneliest day of the week.'

'Sounds like a song,' Dawn commented.

'Even a film,' added Natasha.

'The story of my life without Joe,' reflected Louise. 'It would open with me letting torn photos of our first kiss in the Haunted House at Alton Towers slip through my fingers to be swept away by the river,' she sighed deeply.

Natasha and Dawn winced at the memory of

Louise on the suspension bridge 'discarding her memories' of Joe by throwing torn photos into the river.

'I think it would be very therapeutic for you to write it down,' Maddie said. Louise looked at her suspiciously but decided she was being genuine.

'It would also be good for you to come with us today. Lay the ghost so to speak,' Dawn suggested, solicitously.

Louise looked thoughtful. 'What do you think, Natasha?'

Natasha nodded her agreement, trying to suppress a laugh. 'We'll see you through the pain.'

Louise thought again and, after agonizing, made the decision they all expected to hear – she would come along, too. The boys had now arrived and were making their way through the pub garden. Tony was trying to tell Kurt about the Video Road Race Competition but quickly realized that Kurt's attention was focused elsewhere.

Tony continued, 'Courtney Love was at the college signing on for a welding course. Said she was fed up of being a pop goddess,' Tony knew exactly who Kurt was concentrating on. 'You're not listening to a word I'm saying, are you?'

'Yes,' said Kurt. 'Welding.' Then as a greeting, trying to act as if it was no big deal he looked at Natasha, 'Natasha.'

'Hi Benson. Looking forward to your big day out?'

'I managed to sleep.'

Natasha allowed him a grudging smile and then began to organize the transport – who should go in Maddie's car and who in Bazz's van. It was finally agreed that Natasha, Dawn, Sarah and Cindy should go in Maddie's car and Kurt, Tony, Julie, Jambo and Max with Bazz.

'M56, M6 down to junction 15 then just follow the signs – or just follow us,' said Kurt, when Maddie asked about the route.

'Follow Bazz's rust bucket? Get real. We'll see you at the Monorail entrance,' said Maddie.

With everyone happy they moved towards the vehicles. Except for one person who was left sitting behind at the tables alone. Naturally it was Louise. Fortunately Dawn noticed and with a diplomatic cough reminded Natasha who smiled apologetically. Unfortunately, there was not enough room for Louise in Maddie's car and she found herself sitting glumly and uncomfortably on a box of Bazz's gear sandwiched between Max and Jambo. Tony and Julie were opposite, fondly looking at the photograph of themselves and Kurt was in the passenger seat next to Bazz. And so they set off.

Chapter 7

The girls in Maddie's car were in high spirits, chatting and joking. They were all looking forward to their day.

'I hope they're looking after Louise in her delicate state,' giggled Dawn.

'Don't have any doubts about that,' said Natasha. 'I've told Benson if he ever wants me to speak to him again nothing must go wrong today, particularly with getting Louise there.'

The others looked impressed that Natasha could lay down the law with Kurt.

'So what did he say?' asked Dawn.

'That's cool,' Natasha did a fair impersonation of Kurt, making the others laugh.

'He may be cool but he's on heat when it comes to you,' said Dawn.

Natasha looked unimpressed. Her expression said 'isn't everyone?' Maddie decided to tease her a little.

'I heard Kurt talking to someone,' she said to Natasha. 'It must have been about you. He said that the only girl he could ever really fall for would have to be stunningly good-looking.'

Natasha remained coolly nonchalant but listened closely to every word. 'She'd have to have an outstanding personality and be really sexy.' By now Natasha was openly smiling. Maddie concluded, 'Either that, or her dad would have to own a pub.'

The others fell about laughing, while Natasha made a comic attempt to hit Maddie. In that good-natured atmosphere they travelled on.

In the van everyone but Louise was having fun. Jambo was showing the others his copy of *Viz*.

'You actually sent a top tip into *Viz*?' Kurt looked at him in stunned amusement. 'Why?'

Jambo grinned and read it aloud, 'Brilliant isn't it? "*Top tips from* Viz. *To save time and effort flavouring your chips, why not dilute salt in the vinegar then you only have to make half the effort. Jambo Bolton, Chester*." I could revolutionize the condiment industry.'

The lads cheered. Louise looked bored.

'Your slogan could be: *Worth the effort, for only half the effort*,' Bazz suggested.

'Just be the driver and don't lose the girls,' Kurt told Bazz, he was determined that nothing should go wrong today.

Bazz drove on and continued to scan the airwaves for Whistle Blower. He at last had some success and let out a whoop of delight which shocked Louise into taking notice.

'What's he talking about?' she asked.

'A UFO,' Bazz was absolutely certain.

Kurt yawned and looked out of the window. Louise looked stunned and impressed.

Meanwhile the girls had stopped for petrol. Sarah and Cindy dashed off to the shop for something to eat.

'We're all going to stick together, aren't we?' said Natasha.

'That's the deal,' Dawn nodded.

'It had better be,' said Maddie. She grinned at Dawn, "Cause if you and Jambo pair off and Natasha and egoman . . .'

'You must be joking,' replied Dawn. Natasha dismissed the whole idea with a laugh.

'. . . There will only be me, Sarah and Cindy in the car going home, get my meaning?' Maddie continued.

Dawn and Natasha shared a mock-worried look. They all laughed as Sarah and Cindy returned and they set off again, with Maddie determined to beat the boys to Alton Towers.

In Bazz's van Louise had taken over tuning the scanner. She was as intrigued and excited by Whistle Blower's broadcasts as Bazz. Tony thought it might be a satellite that had gone out of control, Kurt still thought it was all a hoax and Jambo had started going on about aliens again. Bazz was still utterly convinced that it was all genuine.

'Whistle Blower's into a channel restricted to

military use only. It's impossible to broadcast on it,' he argued.

'How come you can listen to it then?'

'I can listen but not transmit,' Bazz explained. Whistle Blower's voice crackled over the scanner. 'Listen, there's something really heavy going down.'

'Confirmation of grounded "object" in a field in Somerford, Cheshire,' the voice announced. There was open-mouthed astonishment from everyone in the van.

'Somerford is just down the road,' exclaimed Jambo. Tony checked the map, they were very close.

'No confirmation yet on extra-terrestrial biological entities, that's alien life forms to you and me folks. They're saying this is a classified broadcast. Code "Visiting Stranger" to be initiated. I'll stay on the air as long as I can but I'm on my way to Somerford,' Whistle Blower sounded excited.

'So are we,' said Bazz.

'No, it's a hoax!' Kurt was firm. 'It has to be!'

'Don't be so negative,' said Louise as keen to investigate as Bazz. 'There's overwhelming evidence of a cover up in the US about the landing in Roswell.'

Kurt gave her an extremely cynical look.

'That's the turn-off ahead,' said Tony.

'Take it!' ordered Louise.

'Don't you dare!' Kurt was adamant.

'Take it!' Bazz wavered, unsure what to do,

so Louise made his mind up for him by grabbing the steering wheel. The van rocked and tilted alarmingly to one side before righting itself – on the road to Somerford. Kurt looked furious and Louise triumphant, choosing to ignore the fact that she had almost killed everyone or at the very least caused a serious accident. Louise seemed oblivious to the angry sound of other drivers' horns but even Bazz looked shocked.

The girls waited at the monorail station as they had agreed, growing increasingly impatient to go on into the park.

'We've waited long enough, come on,' Natasha said finally. 'That stupid van'll have broken down.'

'We may as well go into the park and take the chance of them catching up with us,' Maddie added. The others reluctantly agreed and they boarded the waiting monorail.

'We should have known Benson and Co would make a mess of the day,' Natasha sounded fed up.

'Hope Julie and Louise are all right with them,' said Dawn.

'Probably stuck in some lay-by somewhere – bored to death.'

The others were actually making their way through some woods to where they thought the action was. Bazz was carrying his scanner.

'Why're we looking for alien life forms when

we've brought our own anyway? Together with his very own UFO,' Kurt meant Bazz and his scanner.

'Don't you have any curiosity?' asked Jambo.

'Yeah – about how long it'll take us to reach Alton Towers,' Kurt had a horrible, sinking feeling that Natasha would blame him for their lateness. The day was going to be a disaster. The sight of Tony and Julie, cuddling and lagging behind, added to Kurt's frustration.

'We could make a fortune, Kurt. Every newspaper in the country'd buy our story,' said Jambo.

'First there has to be a story,' Kurt pointed out. 'We're here on the say so of one radio-ham nut.'

'Whistle Blower's come up with good stuff in the past few weeks,' Bazz fiddled with the scanner.

'Little green men from Mars? Come on!'

'You took the ouija board seriously, why not this?' asked Louise.

Of course, Kurt could not answer truthfully. He sighed, realizing he had to go along with it. A little later, Bazz spotted police cars in the distance. He was sure this was the right place. Everyone except Kurt looked excited.

'This whole thing's mad,' Kurt groaned. 'What am I doing here? I don't believe in flying saucers.'

'What about the Roswell incident then?' demanded Louise. Jambo looked puzzled and

Louise was only too happy to give him the details. 'In 1947 a UFO crashed in New Mexico complete with bodies. One alien was even alive. There were too many witnesses for it not to be true and there's a film of an alien autopsy.'

'I saw that. The film was obviously a wind-up with clever special effects. You've seen too many episodes of *The X Files*,' Kurt was still sceptical.

'The transmission we heard has to be right,' Bazz pointed to his crackling scanner. 'I shouldn't even be listening to these wave-bands.'

They walked nervously on along a path between trees. Tony and Julie did not look too bothered about what was going on around them as they stopped to kiss. Suddenly Louise screamed. A man wearing an anorak stepped out of the shadows in front of them. He gestured for them to be quiet and to follow him.

'Where to?' Kurt was suspicious.

'We've set up a base. You're part of a very privileged minority.'

Intrigued and excited, the rest of the group followed. Kurt hesitated.

'How do we know who he is?' Kurt muttered.

'Or what,' said Tony. Kurt just looked at him. 'It is possible – we can't be the only ones in the entire universe.'

'Get real,' Kurt pulled a face. Jambo, Bazz and Louise were all eagerly following the man and Kurt reluctantly trailed behind. Tony and Julie stopped once more, staring deeply into each others' eyes before Tony pulled Julie, smiling, towards him. They soon lost sight of the others.

The man led the way to a camouflaged green net. 'In there,' he said. 'We have to log the identities of all witnesses.' Their eager anticipation soon evaporated as they stepped into a tent to see a queue of similar UFO spotters lining up to give their particulars to the police. The truth dawned on them at the same moment – it was a set-up. They turned to flee and saw a wall of four police officers close the gap behind them. The trap had snapped shut.

'Great,' muttered Kurt. 'The biggest alien life form of them all!'

The man who had led them to the tent merely smiled, 'Welcome to Operation "Venus" Flytrap!'

Kurt glared at Jambo and Bazz in a way that they knew was building to a volcanic-sized eruption.

'Look,' said Jambo, trying to keep the peace. 'We all decided to . . .'

'Don't say one more word,' Kurt was still glaring at them. Louise went to speak. 'Don't!' She didn't.

Twenty minutes later they were still waiting to have their details taken.

Louise was indignant. 'This is – ridiculous.'

'It's worse than that. This has got to be the most embarrassing thing that's ever happened to me,' Kurt gazed round at the other, mainly anorak-clad would-be UFO spotters.

'It's all right for the rest of you,' said Bazz. 'I could get all my gear confiscated.'

'Good!' Kurt sounded bitter.

The original anoraked policeman they had followed returned with a clipboard.

'What's going to happen to us?' asked Louise.

'I'm just a storm trooper supporting the Empire against you Jedis. You'll have to ask Darth Vader what your punishment will be. Perhaps you'll just be thrown to Jabba the Hutt, if you're lucky,' he sounded bored, but could not suppress a smile.

'You're loving this, aren't you? We're supposed to be on our way to meet someone,' Kurt paused and looked derisively at Bazz, 'And it wasn't little green men in flying saucers!'

'You shouldn't have been listening to classified frequencies then, should you?' anorak man sneered.

'It sounded real. You can't blame me,' Bazz said, miserably.

'Don't feel so bad about it, son. We always get a good turn-out for this. Our little version of "may the force be with you". Get it?' anorak grinned.

Kurt gave him a sarcastic smile. Louise decided to try a different approach, 'How long is all this going to take? My mother's a solicitor, you know.' She was silenced by a warning look from the others not to wind the guy up.

'Then you should have more respect for the law . . . even if it is alien to you! And we won't be long now. We just want to take your details. What planet you're from, that sort of thing,' Louise visibly shrank.

Kurt shook his head, hardly believing the situation he found himself in. 'How bad can this get?' he wondered, under his breath.

Eventually all their details were taken and the man led Kurt and the others back to where he found them and where they had left Tony and Julie. They seemed not to have missed the others as they were still practising the kiss of life. The anorak man looked but ignored them.

'Natasha is never going to believe this,' Kurt sighed.

'You can always show her the certificate we give you to say you've had the pleasure of meeting aliens,' the man suggested. 'To everybody else, it'll look like a Caution letter – but you'll know what it really is.'

'This could all be a cover-up, couldn't it?' said Louise. The others, including the anorak man, looked at her, not believing that she could be serious. They were absolutely amazed to see that she was – deadly serious.

'This might be an exercise to catch people responding to classified frequencies but if there really has been a UFO then this would be the perfect cover story.'

Anorak walked away shaking his head, thinking that he really had seen it all now. Kurt sighed, and pushed Bazz towards the van.

Chapter 8

They arrived at Alton Towers over an hour and a half late. Bazz again delayed them, this time by meticulously threading a heavy-duty chain through the steering wheel as his very own security device. Kurt, looking tense, was counting to ten. Even Jambo grew impatient.

'Bazz,' he reasoned. 'You have to be kidding. The chain's worth more than the van.'

Eventually Bazz finished, padlocked it and they headed off to the monorail station. Kurt was torn between remaining cool and desperately seeking Natasha.

The girls had been having exactly the sort of day out they had planned, albeit without half of their party. After the Runaway Train, they had decided to dare Nemesis. Close to it, watching the reactions of the people already on it, screaming past them at top speed, Natasha, Dawn, Cindy, Sarah and Maddie began to have second thoughts. Dawn had earlier confidently boasted that she was not afraid of any ride in the world but even she began to make excuses about the length of the queue waiting. There were to be no excuses, however, and before long it was their turn to board. Natasha, Maddie and Dawn thought better of sitting in the front seats and chose the second row – Dawn sat in the middle with grave misgivings about what was to come. Cindy and Sarah scrambled into the front row and seemed to be looking forward to the ride with great enthusiasm. Just over a minute later the ride was over. Maddie, Dawn and Natasha climbed out with a mixture of relief and pleasure.

'That was the worst and best moment of my life,' exclaimed Dawn, only slightly exaggerating.

'It was brilliant,' shouted Sarah, with Cindy agreeing.

'Absolutely fantastic. Scariest thing in the whole world,' laughed Maddie.

'I thought it was a bit tame myself,' said Natasha.

'Not!' Maddie and Dawn yelled together. Laughing, they all moved on to try the River Rapids.

The girls took a break from all the excitement to buy ice creams at about the time that Bazz's party were boarding the monorail. Bazz scrambled to the front arguing that this was the best position from which to look out for the girls. Unfortunately he had muddled which way the train would be going and they were actually at the back. Bazz gave a wimpish 'sorry' gesture and slunk away to find a seat. Kurt looked like thunder. Jambo tried to pat his shoulder to reassure him but Kurt just glared first at his hand and then at Jambo himself. Jambo shrugged and looked at Louise, who coldly looked away, again bored with the company. Max gazed out of the window and Tony and Julie gazed at each other.

Bazz, sitting miserably alone by the window was the first to spot the girls – happily eating their ice creams as the monorail passed overhead. Everyone tried to attract their attention but the girls strolled obliviously onwards to the Haunted House.

'I bet Kurt was looking forward to going in here with you,' smiled Maddie.

'But as neither Kurt nor his cronies are around we can go in ourselves and enjoy it,' Natasha replied. 'Not too scary for you, Dawn?'

'Plastic skeletons and a few old dishcloths dangling down? I've been on Nemesis, nothing can scare me now,' Dawn was scathing.

At last inside the park, Kurt and Tony studied a map.

'There's a couple of top tips in here as well, Jambo,' Tony grinned. '"Bring your camera and catch your day on film and look out for your photographs at the end of rides".'

'Here's another. Don't listen to mates who are prats about flying saucers,' Kurt was not joking.

'I still think it could be a big cover up,' Louise

said. She was silenced by hostile looks, not just from Kurt, but from everyone. She wandered away alone getting lost in her own thoughts. Kurt's thoughts were still on Natasha and how to catch up with her. He knew Natasha was keen to go on Nemesis and the girls had seemed to be heading in that direction. Tony announced he and Julie were going off by themselves.

'We'll all get split up,' Kurt protested.

'We'll meet you by the Tea Cup ride in an hour,' Julie suggested.

'And a half,' Tony added.

Kurt was about to make for the sky ride when he realized Louise was looking slightly emotional. 'Are you O.K.?'

'Yes,' Louise sighed, dramatically. 'I was just thinking of the last time I was here – another world. You go on – I'll meet you at the Tea Cups,' she quickly made for the Ladies.

Kurt shrugged and hurried after the others. There was little he could do to cheer her up.

The girls, looking shocked but happy, had finished their journey through the Haunted House and agreed on a rest and a drink . . . but only after the Log Flume. As Kurt, Jambo, Max and Bazz walked under the Flume reading their Alton Towers' guide, the girls passed overhead. Neither group noticed the other. Everyone in Kurt's party was hungry and wanted to eat except Kurt who wanted to find the girls first.

Kurt reluctantly agreed to go off on his own while the others got something to eat and to meet later at the Tea Cups. Unbeknown to him, a little later, Julie and Tony, walking into one of the cafes met the girls who were just about to leave. Tony and Julie were too wrapped up in each other to explain much.

Kurt, meanwhile, was thoroughly miserable on his own. He didn't realize it, but he kept just missing Natasha and the others. He watched the River Rapids as the girls passed overhead on the Skyride but they did not see him nor he them. At the agreed time, Kurt arrived at the Tea Cup ride. No one else showed up. At that moment, Jambo was putting his top tip into practise, dissolving salt in the vinegar and pouring it liberally on to his second portion of chips. Kurt eventually found Jambo, Max, Bazz and Louise but saw no sign of the girls. Miserably he joined his party on the monorail to head back to the van. As far as he was concerned, the day had been a disaster.

The girls had thoroughly enjoyed the day, they had collected masses of souvenirs and felt tired and happy. They clambered down from the monorail on the way to the car park. Sarah and Cindy bounded happily ahead. Dawn nodded towards Sarah, 'Well, it worked. One sister out of her shell and in touch with the world again.'

'Yeah, for her,' there was a hint of disappointment in Natasha's voice. Despite the fact that she had really had a good time, not everything had worked out entirely as she hoped or expected. 'What happened to Benson and Louise?'

Dawn nudged Natasha. They were surprised to see Kurt and the others getting off at the other end of the monorail. It took some time to explain the reason for their delayed arrival at Alton Towers and Natasha and the girls had difficulty taking everything in. Various bits had to be repeated and matters were not helped by Louise generally complicating the story.

'How many moons does your planet have?' asked Natasha incredulously.

'It could have been a UFO and the whole story a cover-up,' Louise insisted.

'I've never heard anything so ridiculous in all my life,' said Dawn.

'The whole thing is true – everything but the obvious!' Kurt protested. 'Now can we try to salvage what's left of the day by going to have a drink or something?'

'I'd rather get straight home – there's too many memories here for me,' said Louise resolutely. She strode off purposefully towards Maddie's car.

That was all Kurt needed to finish everything off. Natasha was about to follow Louise when Kurt gave it one more try.

'Hey, Natasha,' he called. 'We can't go on not meeting like this.'

'It'd help if we could get on the same

timescale, even the same planet,' Natasha snapped. 'Get your act together, Benson.'

Kurt looked despondent. He had known he would get the fallout, even though he was the only one who had not been taken in by the UFO hoax, and had not wanted to investigate. 'I guess I won't get the chance to explain properly,' he thought. The day seemed to sum up his relationship with Natasha pretty well.

Perhaps Natasha sensed something of this. She stopped and softened the blow by saying, 'We could all go back to my dad's place, of course – that's if you can manage to arrive before closing time.' She smiled at Kurt.

Kurt grinned, feeling more philosophical. Perhaps the day didn't have to be a total washout – yet. Unfortunately for Kurt the hope was shortlived. The girls had disappeared from view and everyone else clambered into the van and settled down for the drive home. Bazz checked his pockets, checked them again and with mounting panic got out of the van and hunted through for a third time. He then frantically scanned the floor of the van and the ground all around it. At last he had to accept the fact that he no longer had the key to his padlock and the chain wound so thoroughly around the steering wheel.

'I think it might be on Nemesis,' Bazz grimaced.

Chapter 9

Christmas was fast approaching and everyone was making plans. Kurt was set on a New Year's party where he could again try to make a move on Natasha. After the Alton Towers fiasco they had both been acting coolly towards one another but there was no denying the fact that Kurt was still mad about the girl and he even dared to suspect that Natasha felt much the same about him. Kurt had never liked anyone else so much before – or failed to get anywhere after such a long time. Still, Christmas and the New Year should be just the time to make his move. Always assuming that his mum and dad went away, as usual.

Kurt's plans were to receive a minor setback. After a fairly riotous evening, Kurt was woken for the fifth day in a row at 6.59 a.m. by an electronic alarm. As before, he sprang out of bed to try to locate the source of the sound but before he could, the noise stopped. Kurt groaned and tried to go back to sleep but it was difficult with Jambo's feet under his nose. As a result, when his mother appeared to wake him, Kurt was already in the bathroom cleaning his teeth. Mrs Benson opened the blinds and gasped to see an 'alien' on the pillow where Kurt's head should be. Kurt rushed in to see what the commotion was about and saw Jambo pulling off the mask and grinning, bleary-eyed. Mrs Benson was not impressed. She turned, tight-lipped to Kurt.

'Your father and I are trying to decide what we're going to do for New Year and whether or not you're trustworthy enough to be left on your own.'

Kurt mumbled through his toothbrush and, after wiping toothpaste from her face, Mrs Benson added, indicating Jambo, 'And that never exactly strengthens your case does it?' She left.

'Nice one, Jam . . .'

A little later, Jambo was dressed and looking 'normal' and Kurt returned with two mugs of coffee.

'Any luck with the hunt for the unidentified bleeping object this morning?'

Kurt shook his head. 'One of these days I'll find it and smash it to pieces – and if my New Year's Eve bash is cancelled, then you and that mask will be in the frame. They were actually going to let me off the annual family pilgrimage to my grandparents' and let me have a party.'

'Don't worry – the rest of us could have a party round my house,' Jambo grinned cheerfully at Kurt's despondent look. 'My mum's cool, but anyway she's off to my auntie's in

America for Christmas. I'm taking her to the airport later.'

'Christmas!' exclaimed Kurt. 'I've got to do my Christmas shopping later. How come you're not going with her?'

'I've got things to do,' Jambo grinned.

'I'm surprised you and your mum recognize each other.'

'We work together, that's enough for anyone.'

'I wouldn't recognize her. What things to do?'

Jambo refused to elaborate, which puzzled Kurt. 'Things worth missing a freebie trip to the States for?'

'I was banking on an invitation here for my Christmas dinner like last year. She cooks a mean roastie, your mum.'

Kurt just looked at Jambo as if he should be so lucky. While shopping in Chester later that evening, Kurt thought he had discovered a surprising clue to Jambo's evasiveness about his Christmas plans. He was just paying for a shirt at the counter when he saw Jambo on the opposite side of the street, laden with shopping. Kurt finished paying and hurried outside to catch up with him but just as he did a car pulled up next to Jambo and an attractive, glamorous woman got out and helped Jambo unload his shopping into the boot. She kissed him quickly on the cheek and they both climbed into the car. Kurt was beside himself with curiosity. Who was that?

Dawn was eating breakfast and reading the newspaper when Terry walked in. He laughed as she hastily pulled her dressing gown up to her neck and then he whisked the paper away.

'Hey – I was reading that!' Dawn protested.

Terry just grinned maliciously, 'I don't pay to have it delivered so you can read it.'

Fortunately, he was out of the way getting dressed when Natasha arrived. She had been worried when she rang the shop and Maddie's mother had told her Dawn was away sick.

'I'm fine. I just didn't want to leave Max and Cindy on their own with you know who,' Dawn said in a hushed voice. 'Mum's due back in an hour so I'll just go in late.'

'You shouldn't have to let all this rule your life,' Natasha was sympathetic.

Dawn shrugged. She didn't know what else she could do. 'Can we talk about something else please?' said Dawn, switching into gossip mode. 'What about you and Benson?'

Natasha took a deep breath, 'I've decided to give him some more encouragement.'

'You mean like when you invited him to Alton Towers and spent the whole day missing each other?'

'Tell me about it,' Natasha pulled a face. 'This time it'll be different, it'll be under controlled conditions – I thought I'd invite him over to the pub on Christmas night. Dad's only open for friends and regulars. I'm sure even

Benson will get the message if I invite him personally.'

Before Dawn could answer they were interrupted by Terry. He sauntered in and almost licked his lips at the sight of Natasha.

'Girls-talk, hey? Can I listen,' he drooled.

Both girls totally ignored Terry as they left the room.

'It's not for lower primates,' Dawn said coldly.

Natasha had to leave for her last college classes before Christmas and Dawn killed time waiting for her mother to return, flicking through a magazine and watching TV with Max. On his way through, Terry decided that he wanted to watch the American football and switched to the video channel. Both Dawn and Max protested which simply seemed to please Terry.

'Tough – this should be a good game.' He pressed play and the opening credits to Brookside began to roll. Puzzled, Terry pressed forward search. Dawn laughed behind her magazine. There was no sign of Terry's NFL and he looked angrily at Dawn and Max. 'Who's taped over my football? Was it you?' he accused Max, who looked the guiltier out of the two.

'It was an accident. Dawn asked me to tape Brookie for her – I thought it was a blank tape, there was nothing written on it,' Max protested.

Terry stood up and crossed over to Max leaning down over him so they were face to face.

'You little moron, can't you do anything right?' Terry hissed poking Max, hard.

'Get off me.'

'Leave him alone,' said Dawn.

'It's about time you started showing me a bit more respect you little brat!' Terry yelled.

'Why? You're not my dad!'

'I wouldn't wanna be that drip!'

'I'm glad I taped over your stupid American football,' Max faced Terry as he stood to leave.

Now really angry, Terry cursed Max and slapped him across the head. Dawn sprang from the sofa to stand between Terry and Max who was on the verge of tears. 'Don't you dare lay a finger on him!' she yelled back.

Angela, who had just that moment arrived back, rushed into the room to see what all the noise was about.

'He hit Max,' Dawn pointed at Terry.

'Yes, I'm sorry, I lost it. But he was answering back and being cheeky,' Terry was defensive and overly concerned.

'He wasn't!' Dawn was angry – she again pointed at Terry. 'He was being horrible.'

'I think you've said enough. If you didn't interfere maybe there wouldn't be this sort of trouble,' Angela said.

Dawn didn't know how to convince her mother about Terry. She stormed angrily out.

Kurt had tackled as much of his Christmas shopping as he could bear and with nothing else planned he decided to take his hot gossip about Jambo to Tony. He waved at Tony through the window and met him in the canteen entrance.

'Guess who I've just spotted playing the toy-boy about town?' Kurt said salaciously. 'With the glamorous Ms X.'

Tony was intrigued but hadn't a clue who it could be.

'Jambo, no less. He was carrying all her shopping and getting kissed for doing it,' Kurt went on, pleased with the reaction his news was getting.

'I bet she's some rich, frustrated housewife whose husband's always on business,' Tony speculated, his mind going into overdrive.

'You reckon?'

'And starved of love and attention, she's turned for comfort to the handsome young man who delivers her plants . . .' Tony's fantasy was running away with him.

Kurt might ordinarily have been more dismissive but he was enjoying it too much, 'Bedding plants?' Tony and Kurt broke into fits of laughter at this. On a more sober note Kurt told Tony the possible bad news about New Year, 'The New Year's Eve bash at Benson Towers was thrown into serious jeopardy this morning by a lethal mixture of scary mask and one strung-out mother.'

'And a hint of Jambo?' was Tony's educated guess.

'Got it in one. It's all right for Lady

Chatterley's lover, he looks well sorted for his Christmas box. I should know later today if it's on or not,' Kurt said.

Tony had to get back to work, grimacing at the depressing picture inside the canteen. Still, after today he would have a two-week break from students and their wacky behaviour. 'Looks like someone wants a word with you. Good luck,' Tony grinned.

Kurt was surprised to see Natasha walking towards him and slightly suspicious when she hesitantly began speaking, 'If I invite you somewhere, you won't turn it into another fiasco like Alton Towers?'

'That was Bazz's fault – anyway it depends what it is,' there had been so many false starts and hopeful beginnings, that Kurt couldn't help being wary.

'It's taking a lot to say this, Benson,' Natasha said seriously. 'What are you doing on Christmas night?'

Now Kurt really was surprised. 'Nothing,' he said enthusiastically, then tried to sound more casual. 'Nothing planned anyway – how about you?'

'Dad's opening the pub for friends and regulars, I wondered if you fancied coming?'

Kurt was really pleased – a fact which Natasha noted. 'Well you are a regular aren't you?' she asked with a wry smile.

Kurt grinned, 'Me – and the guys?' Natasha nodded. 'Although I think Jambo might have other things on his mind.' Natasha looked suitably intrigued and Kurt continued conspiratorially. 'It looks like our Jambo is the secret toy boy of a glamorous, mystery woman.'

'You sound envious – fancy an older woman yourself do you?'

'No, I prefer the more immature type myself,' Kurt smiled into her grey eyes.

Natasha tried to hide her amusement and rolled her eyes at him. Kurt was in such a good mood after this invitation that when he got home, he felt inspired to work on his latest composition – a rock ballad called 'It sounds so simple'. Unfortunately Ollie appeared halfway through when Kurt was obliviously singing. He was delighted to detect the word 'love' in the song and decided this was the ideal opportunity to taunt Kurt when he appeared more vulnerable than usual. Kurt was angry to have been caught out and angry with Ollie for coming in without knocking. He lobbed a keyboard instructions book at his younger brother which missed – and very narrowly missed his sister, Lucy, who looked thoroughly unimpressed. They were all wanted for a family conference downstairs.

'There's no way they're gonna let you stay at home,' Ollie taunted Kurt, who launched another book, again missing. Ollie was gloating and Kurt not in the best frame of mind as they trooped downstairs. The roles were soon reversed when Juliet announced they had decided that Kurt could stay behind at New Year and have his party but that Ollie and Lucy had to go to Stoke and their grandparents as usual.

There was, however, a sting for Kurt. His father reeled off the two conditions of this privilege. The first was that Kurt pay for any damage from the party and the second was that he stayed in for the family gathering with Aunt Rose on Christmas Day – and night.

'No problem,' said Kurt, smugly. Then he realized. 'Christmas night, as in Christmas Day night? I can't – I've already got something arranged.'

But his parents wouldn't budge. 'Either you stay here with us at Christmas or you can forget New Year, it's as simple as that.'

Kurt was gutted. There was no point in arguing, he would just have to think of a way around it. He went outside to the garage to work on his car which was almost finished.

Ollie decided to seize the opportunity for revenge on Kurt. Looking shiftily about and being reassured by the sound of the throbbing car engine, Ollie crept into Kurt's room. He made straight for the studio set-up and ejected the tape that Kurt had been playing earlier. He carefully closed Kurt's bedroom door before skulking off towards his own room. His expression changed from one of conniving satisfaction to one of horror as he heard, 'Freeze!' It was Lucy standing at her bedroom door watching him.

'All right, Lucy,' Ollie tried to act casual, but Lucy was not fooled. She wanted to know what he was up to and snatched the tape from his hand.

'Kurt said I could just go in and get it,' Ollie lied, badly.

'So it's O.K. if I go down and ask him then?' Lucy said making to go downstairs. Ollie looked desperate. 'What's on the tape?' Louise asked.

'Just one of his new songs.'

'Why would you risk your life sneaking into Kurt's kingdom just to listen to one of those awful rackets he calls songs?'

Ollie weakly tried to say he just wanted to listen but as he was clearly still lying Lucy demanded the truth immediately, or she would tell Kurt.

'I'm sick of Kurt always getting his own way and pushing everyone around. I just thought I'd bring him down a peg or two,' Ollie sounded aggrieved. He then tried to involve Lucy in his plan, speaking in a hushed, secretive tone. 'This is a soppy love song written by Mr Cool about his heart-throb, Natasha. I thought it would be interesting if a few copies were passed around.'

'That's a bit vindictive isn't it?' Lucy quizzed.

'I owe him one. He made me hand over all my savings to fix up his stupid car.'

'The stupid car you nearly wrote off,' Lucy's mind was made up. 'You've only got your pathetic immaturity to blame for all that. I'm not surprised he made you pay up – I would have too.'

'You're just like everyone else. Good old Kurt can't do any wrong,' he was about to walk sulkily back to his room but Lucy grabbed his arm.

'It might be a giggle now but what about when Kurt finds out and comes looking for you?' Ollie cringed and seemed to be getting the point. 'You just be grateful I'm not going to tell him.'

Ollie sloped off. Lucy looked at the tape wondering. Rather nervously, knowing she shouldn't really be listening, Lucy began to play the tape on the cassette player in the kitchen. The song came on halfway through and Lucy could see why Ollie had found it so amusing. She was surprised at the lyrics. Ollie was right – it was a love song from Kurt to Natasha. In the garage Kurt listened to the engine with a satisfied smile. He switched it off and as the engine died, he caught faint snatches of music – very familiar music. He listened intently for a second and bounded towards the kitchen.

It would be difficult to say who looked more shocked and embarrassed. Kurt stabbed the eject button angrily to retrieve his tape.

'I can explain,' Lucy pleaded, looking thoroughly ashamed.

Lucy raced upstairs after Kurt, nipping into his room just before he slammed the door shut. Fortunately for her, the explanation was immediately plausible and it was much easier for

Kurt to imagine Ollie stealing the tape than Lucy.

'I don't see what the problem would have been if people heard it anyway. I think it's a nice song,' Lucy was slightly teasing, but quite serious. 'I didn't know you were such a romantic.'

Kurt was still embarrassed. 'Well, it isn't finished yet and the last thing I want is Ollie promoting my music. Thanks Lucy. I owe you one.'

Chapter 10

Later that afternoon, Natasha was in the middle of her Christmas shopping. Needing a break and finding herself close to the interior design shop where Dawn worked, she decided to call on her friend. There were several potential customers but they were all happy to browse and Dawn ushered Natasha to the far side of the shop pretending she was also a customer.

'What time did you eventually get in this morning?' Natasha asked in a hushed voice, while Dawn held up some fabric for Natasha to inspect.

'About twelve, after I'd managed to stop Terry from beating up Max.'

Natasha was shocked. 'Does your mum know?'

'She came in halfway through and immediately took Terry's side – she won't have anything said against him,' Dawn was obviously still hurt and upset.

Natasha tried to comfort her. Dawn smiled cheerfully at two customers and promised assistance shortly. She continued to 'help' Natasha.

'How did the last day of college go?'

'I saw Benson . . .' Natasha tried to suppress a smile. 'And I invited him.'

'What did he say?' Dawn's hushed voice sounded excited.

'He's coming but he seemed more interested in Jambo's romantic life than his own.' Dawn wanted to know more. 'No one knows who he's seeing. But, it's an older woman according to Kurt.'

'It all sounds rather intriguing,' said Dawn.

Natasha smiled conspiratorially, plotting. 'You get on well with Jambo. Can't you find out who it is?' Dawn looked uncertain. 'Wouldn't you like to know what's going on?'

Persuaded by Natasha's knowing look, Dawn grinned and agreed to call for a friendly chat '. . . about you and Kurt!' but only after she had dealt with the other customers.

Natasha waited patiently until the shop was empty. And then again while Dawn made the phonecall. She sat on one of the sofas, flicking through sample books while Dawn chatted at the other end of the shop. Finally, Dawn had finished. She threw her hands over her face to cover her embarrassment. 'I think I just made a total idiot of myself,' Dawn groaned. Natasha was surprised. Dawn carried on speaking with her eyes closed. 'I think Jambo thought I was asking him out.'

This amused Natasha. 'What did he say?'

'It wasn't what he said, it was what I said –

asking if he was going out with anyone.'

'And is he?'

'No but it didn't stop me asking if he was sure. And then,' Dawn blushed at the memory. 'When he said he was positive I asked him if he would be taking anyone to your pub on Christmas night!' Natasha was now laughing out loud. 'It's not funny!'

'So there's no mystery woman?'

'If there is he's not letting on and what's worse – he thinks I'm after him now,' Dawn shook her head still embarrassed. She slapped Natasha playfully for giggling uncontrollably.

Tony was finishing work on a high note. He had won the next round of the Video Road Race competition against tough opposition and even managed to laugh at the latest expression of student high spirits – his motorbike had been decorated for Christmas with tinsel garlands and glass baubles. He was just stripping them off when Kurt pulled up.

'Good news, Tone. We celebrate the New Year in style – although it looks like you started early,' Kurt did not sound too certain, however. 'There's just one tiny, little thing that needs sorting first.'

'Like what?' Tony was removing the tinsel garlands and draping them around his neck to use elsewhere.

'I've got the choice between an invitation to

spend Christmas night with Natasha or have the party on New Year's Eve!'

'What!?' said Tony when Kurt explained. 'That's hardly one little thing. Just ring Natasha, say you can't make it on Christmas night and invite her to your party.'

Kurt looked really impressed. He could just imagine how it would sound. 'Hi Natasha. Sorry but my parents won't let me go out on our first date. I've got to stay in cos my aunt's visiting – that's really cool! I'm just going to have to hope she comes to the party and forgives me for not going to their pub on Christmas night.'

Tony looked dubious. He reckoned it was highly likely that Kurt was making a big mistake. He couldn't imagine Natasha taking a little thing like being stood up lightly, but sometimes there was no advising Kurt.

'It will be your loss,' Tony warned, draping Kurt with tinsel. 'Have you told Jambo about the party yet?'

'I thought we'd shoot round the garden centre and see if he's back from taking his mum to the airport.'

They sped off to the garden centre where they were in for a surprise. Crossing the car park towards the main building Kurt suddenly stopped and dragged Tony back around the corner. They both peered out and watched Jambo with his mystery woman getting into a car.

'The sly dog.'

'Where's he off to then?'

'There's only one way to find out – follow that Jambo!'

They followed the car back to Jambo's flat.

'Do you think she's brought him back to her house?' Tony asked, speculating.

'This is Jambo's.'

'No kidding! I've never been here.'

Kurt grinned mischievously. 'It seems rude being so close to his house and not calling in don't you think? Since he spends most of his time in our houses he can hardly mind.'

Tony grinned in agreement. They began to walk along the drive. There was no one about. 'All quiet. What do you think, should we knock on the front door or do it Jambo-style and go straight round to his bedroom?'

They grinned and the decision was made. In cautious anticipation, Kurt and Tony crept down the steps leading to Jambo's flat and the French windows into his bedroom. There was no one about apart from Margaret the cow. Kurt reached forward to knock on the glass when Jambo suddenly appeared giving them a fright. He opened the door and looked curiously at the tinsel. Kurt offered him a strand. 'Merry Christmas. We just thought we'd give you a knock,' Kurt scanned the room, looking for Ms X.

Tony also strained to look inside, but slightly more subtly. 'Seeing we were passing,' he added.

Jambo invited them in, looking slightly mystified. Tony looked around curiously. Jambo had the garden flat which connected with the one above where his mother lived. He had basically been coming and going as he pleased ever since he discovered the mobility of his own legs, alcohol and women. The kitchen area, set in the corner near the French windows was a mess of mugs, coffee and milk, Tony noted, but the rest of the room had been well thought out and planned. Most of the equipment was dated but it had been cleverly recycled and laid out. Jambo had even used old doors and packing cases and material salvaged from the garden centre. The room definitely had a certain style about it and it was more orderly than Tony would have expected. Even Jambo's Liverpool football posters and memorabilia like cup final tickets and film posters were fixed to a large cork board. Tony looked at the school sports trophies, a rowing oar and a parking meter, which Jambo had 'liberated' from somewhere. There was also a child's rocking horse.

Jambo meanwhile was looking at Kurt and Tony expectantly.

'Not disturbing anything are we?' Kurt tried hard to keep a straight face. Tony just burst out laughing. Jambo was totally thrown. Anything he might have said was cut short as the mystery woman walked in wearing a short revealing dressing gown. She looked surprised, but not half as much as Kurt and Tony who stared open-mouthed.

'I'm sorry, I didn't know you had company,' the woman left quickly, looking very self-conscious about her attire.

'No wonder you didn't want to go away for Christmas,' Kurt muttered, looking amazed.

Jambo suddenly realized what must be going through his friends' minds, especially when Tony asked in a concerned voice, 'Do you know what you're doing?'

'It could be fun now, Jam . . . but it could get really heavy,' Kurt added. 'Especially if she's married.'

'Well, divorced,' Jambo said, calmly.

'Has she got any kids?'

'Yes.'

'Oh my god, you've got to be careful. It could get really messy,' Tony sounded shocked.

'You saw her, it's worth the risk – not a touch of jealousy in there is there?' Jambo grinned.

'It can get very messy with kids and ex-husbands,' Kurt warned.

'Is this another of your seminars on how to treat women?'

'Are you sure you're not making a mistake?' Tony's face was a picture of concern.

Jambo decided enough was enough. 'Let me introduce you all properly.' He left to fetch the woman.

Tony turned to Kurt in horror. Kurt shrugged. 'It was you that told me all about the irrationality of sexual chemistry.'

'But that was me and Julie – not me and

Julie's aunt.'

Jambo came back in with the woman, now dressed. 'Kurt, Tony – this is Janice . . . my mother,' Jambo had an amused glint in his eye.

Tony and Kurt again stood open-mouthed, trying not to stare.

Chapter 11

It was Christmas Day and Jambo was completing his festive preparations, decorating an artificial Christmas tree with baubles, tinsel and a complete set of lights. He carefully carried the tree outside to mount it on the top of his mother's car. He rested the tree on a cloth and tied it in place with string. The final touch was a set of PA speakers also tied firmly to the car roof and attached to the line output of a small portable CD player. The tree now had its own Christmas music accompaniment. Jambo stood back to admire the effect and looked delighted with the result. With music still playing, Jambo drove off – attracting a fair amount of attention from passers by who smiled and waved.

At about the same time Tony rushed outside to try out his Christmas present – an Abus Granit lock and bike chain – on his bike. It looked slightly out of place on his small Honda, but Tony was pleased. He was looking forward to seeing Julie later and giving her the silver locket he had bought.

Dawn, Cindy, Max and their mother had a happy hour opening presents without Terry, who was still in bed. The living room was soon in a chaos of destruction as parcels were ripped open and contents admired. Cindy sat in the middle of the destruction, cocooned in a Walkman world, assembling a glass lamp with a hanging bead shade. Max wore roller blades and a cycle crash helmet with his pyjamas while playing on a new Sega Saturn system. Dawn smiled as she stepped through the debris to retrieve a couple of unopened presents from beneath the tree. As she did, Terry walked in behind her, stopping to admire Dawn as she bent to retrieve the gifts. He lolled against the door frame watching. Dawn straightened and noticed Cindy's eyes fixed on the doorway. She turned and her smile faded.

'Did you get anything nice?' Dawn did not reply but held his mocking stare. Max and Cindy watched to see what would happen next. The mood was broken as Angela appeared behind Terry and handed him a mug of coffee.

Mindful of Terry, Dawn stooped carefully to pick up two gifts – one she handed to her mother and the other she threw at Terry who spilt his coffee trying to catch it. He was completely taken by surprise by this. Dawn hurried away to get dressed.

Later, by luck or timing, Terry again walked in when Dawn was leaning over to pick something up. This time they were alone.

'You should be careful about doing that. You could have an accident,' he said.

Dawn jumped and straightened immediately. 'Only if you were around.'

'That wouldn't be an accident – it would be an experience,' Terry grinned.

'Like going to the dentist?' Dawn glared at Terry and was about to leave when he stepped in front of her. He held up the cufflinks he was wearing which had 'No Entry' traffic signs on them. They were Dawn's present to him.

'Thanks,' he said. 'Bit of symbolism is it?'

'At least some parts of your brain work normally,' Dawn said, coldly.

'I take it I'm not going to get a Christmas kiss, then?' Terry grinned at Dawn's appalled expression.

Natasha's day had also started early. She returned to her room from a present-opening session laden with boxes, wrapping paper and a stack of new clothes which she dropped on to the bed with a smile of satisfaction. She leaned towards the mirror to try on a new pair of earrings. The look of pleasure faded as she caught sight of the paper pinned to her notice board and read 'Kurt 634569'. She sighed, remembering the one problem she had about the day or rather the evening. She thought about ringing and then decided to delay - she might still work something out. She dressed quickly and hurried downstairs to vacuum the restaurant. Greg was just finishing the clean up in the bar after the previous night's Christmas Eve revelries.

'The restaurant's all done . . .' Natasha paused trying to build up to something. 'Do you want me to go over the floor in here?'

Greg nodded but was far too sharp not to know when his daughter was up to something. 'What are you after?' Natasha looked at him with mock outrage. 'Don't you want to go to Aunt Madge's tonight?' he asked.

Natasha was speechless for a second. Greg grinned. 'Fair enough. You're old enough to make up your own mind. And I've cleared it with your mother.'

'How did you know?'

'Aunt Madge's,' Greg pulled a 'boring' face. 'Why do you think I started opening the pub on Christmas night?' They smiled at their mutual understanding.

There was, however, another aspect of her evening plans that Natasha had still not cleared with her father. After thoroughly hoovering the bar, Natasha began hesitantly, 'As I won't be going to Aunt Madge's . . . and . . . as there won't be many in tonight, I was wondering . . .' Before she could ask, Louise arrived, holding her hands behind her back and looking extremely smug. Greg and Natasha looked at her expectantly but Louise was too excited even to speak.

'Merry Christmas, Louise,' said Greg. Louise's grin just widened as she nodded. Greg nudged Natasha, realizing Louise was waiting for the right question. 'Ask her,' he said – Natasha was still intent on her unasked request. 'Quickly, before she explodes and ruins all our efforts at cleaning the place up.'

'Oh,' said Natasha, slowly understanding. She smiled. 'Go on – what did you get?'

With a tremendous flourish, Louise whipped out a pair of L-plates. It took Natasha a second or two to realize the implications of this but then she screamed and jumped with excitement.

'You got it!' she exclaimed.

Louise nodded excitedly. 'A Renault Clio.'

Greg, realizing this could have serious repercussions, began to sneak away.

'Radio cassette?'

'CD.'

'Brilliant!' Natasha spotted Greg tiptoeing out. 'Father!' she called him back. 'Everyone's getting cars now.'

'No.' In answer to Natasha's hard-done-by face he added. 'I fell for the late night safety line over the mobile phone but cars come under the category of no way!'

'Anything else I can do after the hoovering?' Natasha smiled, as this was an old debate.

'That's not going to soften me up either.'

'I just want the place to look good for all our "friends and regulars" tonight,' Natasha said.

Louise was still smiling at her L-plates and did not pick up on the sensitivity of the moment. 'Yes,' she said. 'It really is good of you to let us bring the crowd.'

Natasha cringed and Greg immediately looked suspicious. 'Could you define "crowd"?'

'One or two,' Natasha started, vaguely, then in answer to Greg's look. 'Six – ish.'

'How many are lads?'

'I've never actually checked. You've always told me not to,' Natasha shrugged.

'Very funny,' Greg sighed. 'All over sixteen?'

'Not mentally,' Louise quipped.

Greg gave up. 'O.K. But soft drinks in here – even if it is Christmas, we're still open to the public!'

Louise looked apologetically at Natasha when Greg left. 'I thought you'd cleared it.'

'I had – almost,' Natasha grinned. 'So you've had a perfect Christmas.'

'And I've got a course of lessons booked!' Louise looked excited again. She teased Natasha. 'All I need now is to see you finally land Benson.'

'Well, tonight's the night – if he turns up!'

Natasha looked more confident than she felt. As soon as Louise left, Natasha hurried to her room and picked up her phone. She then spent several moments just staring at it trying to bring herself to dial. She paced up and down and finally slumped into a chair. She took a deep breath and tried to stop feeling nervous. 'This is ridiculous!' she told herself firmly. 'It's only Benson.' She worked out exactly what she was going to say and feeling calmer she began to dial, but after three digits she panicked. She could not remember the rest of Kurt's number and at first couldn't see the paper where she had written it down. Sighing with relief, she saw it on her notice board, completed dialling and pressed send. She took another deep breath and prepared herself to sound casual and off-hand.

The only person still not awake or joining in the festivities was Kurt. It was actually all part of a carefully worked out strategy aimed at encouraging his mother to allow him out that evening. Indeed, by midday Mrs Benson was feeling agitated at his prolonged lie-in, knowing very well he was sulking and why.

Mr and Mrs Benson had temporarily abandoned peeling vegetables and polishing silver cutlery in order to reminisce fondly about past Christmases when the children were small. They were both looking slightly misty-eyed at the memory when Ollie and Lucy charged through the kitchen arguing, not even noticing their parents in mid-embrace. The silence that followed their departure, was soon broken by the window shooting open. Jambo appeared with a plastic bin bag over his shoulder. He at least looked sorry to have disturbed them.

'Merry Christmas,' he boomed. 'Sorry . . . Is it O.K. if I go up to Kurt?'

'Why spoil the habit of a lifetime?'

Jambo rummaged in his bag and tossed a parcel each to Mr and Mrs Benson and disappeared. He closed the window and appeared to grab the drainpipe to climb skywards. Jambo swiftly opened Kurt's window, popped his head in to shout 'Happy Christmas' Santa-style and swung his bin bag into the room. Kurt ambled in from the bathroom talking to Tony on the phone. Jambo sniggered as he picked up the gist of the conversation about the plans for that evening and Kurt's invitation from Natasha.

'Why still in here? Don't you want to rush down and see if "he's been"?' Jambo asked, throwing Kurt's present to him.

'I'm trying to build up the guilt factor – reckon if I stay up and sulk for another half hour or so the disaster of all mothers will start to weaken.'

'When you finish this mellowing out year and go back to college – don't do psychology,' Jambo didn't rate the chances of Kurt's strategy working too highly.

Kurt opened his present – it was a set of rear Consul decals for his car. He looked really pleased and handed Jambo his gift – a mug with *'No logo required'* printed on the side. Tired of waiting for her son to appear, Mrs Benson finally sent Ollie up to tell him Aunt Rose was on her way. Jambo began dropping hints about an invitation to stay to lunch which Mrs Benson ignored, he also began teasing Kurt about families being together at Christmas.

Kurt glared at Jambo. 'Lunch is cool but

what's the point of everyone being miserable tonight?'

'Is that a threat?' asked Mrs Benson.

'An observation.'

'As in if I don't get my way I'll be miserable and a right pain for everyone else?'

'You could play charades,' Jambo suggested helpfully.

It was at this point that Lucy waltzed in to announce that Aunt Rose had arrived. Mrs Benson looked in dismay at the unpeeled vegetables and unpolished cutlery. There was still masses more to do. She shook her head feeling anxious. Why did Aunt Rose always have to be early? If it came to it, why did her husband always invite his whole family over for Christmas Day? She knew the answer – it was because he liked lots of people for a good old-fashioned family meal. But, Mrs Benson gritted her teeth, it meant an awful lot of work, especially for herself. She studiously omitted to count Mr Benson peeling vegetables. It would be easier if she wasn't so concerned that everything should be just right and she could do without her eldest son giving her grief about a perfectly reasonable request. Mrs Benson scowled at Kurt and ushered everyone but Jambo outside to greet her husband's aunt.

Aunt Rose was in her mid-seventies, still fit and sprightly and driving herself about in her own car. She was quite a formidable and independent lady, her only concession to old age being a walking stick due to arthritis in one knee.

'Merry Christmas,' Mrs Benson smiled.

'Stupid time of the year, people having to be nice to people they don't see from one year to the next,' Aunt Rose commented. Kurt brightened considerably at this and smiled broadly at his mother. 'At least someone has a sense of humour.' Aunt Rose pointed towards Jambo's car with the Christmas tree and speakers parked in the drive. Mrs Benson looked shocked and dashed inside to find Jambo.

'Something I said?' Aunt Rose looked baffled. 'Was I cool or wicked?'

Kurt laughed.

Everyone was in the middle of opening presents – everything from Aunt Rose came from Caernarfon Castle – tea towels, pencils, a book mark, Snowdon Heather aftershave – Kurt was just unwrapping a beeswax candle, also from the castle, when his mobile phone rang. It was Natasha.

'Benson?' she said quickly. 'It's Natasha. Don't forget. Tonight – eight o'clock. Be there or forget it.' She then hung up.

Kurt was surprised and looked bemused. His expression soon turned to one of agony as he heard his mother say, 'We're all staying in tonight for a traditional family evening.'

Jambo was trying to redeem himself for the car by peeling sprouts and offering help generally.

'Grandad and Grandma will be here soon,' Mrs Benson began as an overture to encouraging Jambo to leave.

'Oh good,' smiled Kurt with deliberate unenthusiasm. 'Grandad can tell us all about his pond again. I wonder if he finally cured the algae problem.'

'Lunch will be ready shortly,' Mrs Benson said pointedly, glaring at Kurt. 'So if you have to get home, James . . .'

'Is McDonalds open today?' Jambo asked Kurt.

'You'll be able to get a sandwich at the garage on Links Lane,' Kurt said.

'I've got some beans left over from yesterday. I'll heat them up. Wonder if Mum's enjoying herself in America without me . . . Ah well, suppose I'd better get off,' Jambo sighed.

'All right,' Mrs Benson gave in and tried to hide her smile. 'So long as you help lay the table.'

'Consider it done Mrs B.'

Chapter 12

At six o'clock that evening, Dawn was ready to go to Natasha's. Angela looked at her coat and hesitated. There was obviously something she wanted to say.

'Are you going already?' she asked.

'Yeah,' said Dawn, picking up her present for Natasha. 'I'll probably stay over at Nat's tonight.'

Angela looked awkward, unsure whether to speak or not. Dawn noted her mother's nervousness and felt a sense of foreboding.

'What's wrong?' she asked.

Terry came out of the kitchen and smiling, put his arms around Angela. She seemed to relax a little and leant her cheek against his hand.

'We wanted to wait until Jude arrived this evening, to tell you all.' (Jude was Dawn's younger sister, who lived in London.) Angela looked embarrassed and gave a slight nervous giggle.

'Tell us all what?' Dawn couldn't imagine what her mother was leading up to.

Still Angela hesitated, until Terry decided to break the news himself. 'What your mother is saying is – we're going to get married!'

Dawn, Cindy and Max looked shocked. It was hardly the most welcome of news. By the time Angela had turned fondly away from Terry's gaze Max and Cindy had busied themselves in what they were doing. Only Dawn met her mother's eyes. She was lost for words. This was the last Christmas present in the world she would have wished for but although the idea was about as horrific as terminal cancer she could not bring herself to shatter her mother's moment of joy completely.

'I . . . I don't know what to say,' Dawn said at last, looking away.

'Congratulations is usual,' Terry sounded almost triumphant.

At that moment, Dawn hated him even more than ever. 'Who for though!? I have to go. See you later,' Dawn could not bear to stay any longer. She had to get away before she said too much.

Dawn told Natasha the ghastly news and then studiously set about putting it out of her mind. She began playing around with a small hand-held video camera, trying to take arty shots of Natasha and her room.

'I could make a video diary of tonight – the night Natasha nabbed Benson,' she joked.

'Nat nabs Neanderthal more like,' laughed Natasha.

'I suppose he will come,' speculated Dawn. 'Things always seem to go wrong.'

'He'd better,' Natasha sounded determined.

Kurt was at home pacing the kitchen floor, growing increasingly anxious as time ticked by. In the living room, Grandad was snoring, Mr Benson was dozing, Grandma had disappeared and Mrs Benson was building up the fire. Aunt Rose rummaged in her bag and finally found a photo which she showed to Lucy.

'What do you reckon?' Rose asked. 'Latest boyfriend.'

Lucy looked a little surprised and even Ollie got up from his Pictionary box to sneak a look. Jambo went to find Kurt. He was now sitting on the worktop in the kitchen looking thoroughly miserable.

'I haven't seen much sign of your mother weakening, even when you gave her that piece of Wedgwood,' said Jambo.

'I'm nineteen – she can't stop me if I want to go out and, if I have to choose between Natasha or she who devours her young . . .' Kurt sounded defiant until his mother walked into the kitchen. Kurt instinctively jumped down from the worktop and immediately felt like an idiot for doing so.

'Have you seen your grandmother?' she asked.

'She's a little old lady about this big with grey . . .' Kurt trailed off in response to his mother's look. 'She went for a lie down. I said she could use my room,' he grinned at his mother's horror-struck face. 'But she should check out your space first.'

'There's no point skulking in here. You are staying in. We had an agreement – you stay in tonight and you can have a party at New Year,' Mrs Benson said.

Kurt groaned. 'But I've done everything – lunch, presents, I've kissed Grandma, listened to Grandad, played Pictionary . . . I need some space.'

'And to see Natasha,' Jambo said. Kurt looked as though he did not want this kind of help, but Jambo carried on anyway. 'You must have been there once Mrs B. When you met someone you wanted to be with all the time – who made your heart pound – who made the sun shine when it rained – who made you hear the birds sing . . .'

To his surprise Kurt saw this seemed to be working.

'Didn't you ever feel like that, Mum?'

'Yeah – then I met your father and you came along!'

'But you know what it's like to be in love, Mrs B?'

'I am not in love,' Kurt's response was automatic.

'In that case it'll keep.'

'It's the big date though,' Jambo was doing his best.

'And if she's that keen, she'll wait. Aunt Rose has come a long way to see us . . .'

Ollie appeared at the door with some startling news. Aunt Rose was going home. Mrs Benson rushed to the living room wondering what was wrong.

Aunt Rose simply smiled and offered her the photograph. 'Ever met someone who made your heart beat faster – who made you see the blue in the sky?' Mrs Benson looked suspiciously at Jambo who looked innocent. 'You don't get many chances at my age,' said Aunt Rose heading for her car.

'O.K.' Mrs Benson turned to Kurt. 'You can go and hear the birds sing.'

A delighted Kurt danced Aunt Rose down the steps and to her car.

Maddie and Louise arrived at the pub to find Natasha dressed and ready early, which was an unusual event as Maddie was quick to point out. No one was in any doubt about why. Louise was still excited about her new car and it was only Dawn who was looking down. Natasha and Maddie did their best to cheer her up and Louise drove her mad with promising horoscope predictions for her.

'Come on,' Dawn said. 'Let's go downstairs and at least get you palmed off with Benson.'

'Thanks a lot!' Natasha grinned.

Louise, however, had now moved on to Dawn's Chinese horoscope, 'The dark of night always heralds the brightness of dawn – hey – dawn . . . Dawn!'

Dawn was not impressed. Maddie quickly grabbed her arm to lead her away. 'Chill out. Come and vent it all downstairs.'

'But not too much. And on the other side of the bar – away from me. So I can – well – with – you know . . .' Natasha trailed off, knowing she sounded pathetic. 'I just want it to be right, tonight.'

This at least brought a smile back to Dawn's face.

'Relax!' Natasha was ordered. 'I thought you wanted to be down there first. We'll all be here.'

'Right,' said Natasha. 'It is only Benson after all.' She went to go and then turned swiftly back. 'Is my make-up all right?'

Dawn reassured her and pushed her towards the stairs. She had never seen Natasha so agitated over a guy.

When the girls reached the bar they were rather dismayed to see how few people were there. A couple of men were setting up keyboards, guitars and a PA on the stage, but the pub was almost deserted. The girls felt rather conspicuous standing among the rest of Greg's middle-aged friends and regulars.

Maddie held up her watch. It was new and it kept excellent time and at that precise moment it showed the time as ten past eight. Everyone checked their watches and turned expectantly to Natasha. She hesitated for a moment but she had told Kurt to be on time. Everyone knew that. Her pride was at stake.

'O.K. – let's go,' Natasha made her decision.

'Where?' asked Louise.

'Anywhere where Benson won't be.'

'What about your friends?' asked Greg when he saw Natasha leaving.

'They're coming with me.'

'I meant the boyfriend.'

'I don't have a boyfriend.'

Kurt and Jambo were at that very second speeding towards the pub in Jambo's mother's car and would probably have arrived in time to meet the girls on their way out. Unfortunately, the Christmas tree, lights and Christmas music which were fully in operation caught the attention of a passing police car. They indicated for Jambo to pull over and requested that he take a breath test, convinced that only someone who had been drinking heavily would drive along with such ridiculous paraphernalia on his car. They were allowed to drive on, but without the Christmas tree and music. Kurt could do nothing but clutch the tree and simmer, knowing he was late. He wondered dismally why this always happened when there was any chance of his getting together with Natasha. When they at last arrived at the pub, Kurt leapt out even before the car had come to a complete halt. He dumped the tree on the bonnet and raced towards the pub, only to find the door locked and a hand-written sign on it saying 'Friends and regulars only'. Kurt slumped back against the door wondering if there was a divine conspiracy against him.

The girls had driven to another pub in Chester where Maddie had a friend and a lively party was going on. Natasha looked increasingly preoccupied. She hadn't given Kurt much of a chance – she had only waited ten minutes. He could be there waiting for her now. Deciding that she had to find out one way or another, Natasha grabbed her coat and left. The others came hurrying after her.

Kurt was about to give up when the door opened. Tony and Julie were leaving. 'Tony – I love you,' Kurt exclaimed and dashed inside. The others looked amused and followed. There were now more people in the bar and Kurt began to look around for Natasha.

Greg was on stage announcing that although his old group was a guitar short – because Bobby's hip was playing up again – they would still play a few of their numbers and old hits. He noticed Kurt looking into the booths and broke off to step down and speak to him.

'You blew it, lad,' he said. 'She usually means what she says.' Kurt's face fell. 'But you can handle a guitar, can't you?'

With classic bad timing, Jambo opened the window next to Kurt and proceeded to wriggle

114

through with his tree. He came face to face with Greg whose immediate response was to ban him from the bar. On hearing that he was with Kurt he conceded that Jambo could stay – but only to listen to Kurt play. When Tony and Julie arrived, Jambo was setting up his Christmas tree on a table.

'What's happening?' asked Tony.

'I've got to prostitute my art to stop Jambo getting us all barred,' Kurt explained.

'Give over. You'd prostitute *yourself* to get up on that stage,' Jambo grinned.

'I thought you were all leaving,' said Kurt.

'We were. But we don't want to miss this,' said Tony. 'So you blew it again with Natasha?'

'He's the one who's been blowing it tonight,' Kurt pointed to Jambo, who mimed blowing into the breathalyser bag. Tony looked puzzled. Kurt was no longer so despondent. 'Although Natasha isn't here right now – where does she live?' The other two began to grin. Kurt continued, 'She's got to get home sometime and when she does – I'll be here . . . helping Frank Sinatra over there relive his youth.'

With that Kurt wandered off to pick up and tune the guitar.

Like Kurt minutes before, Natasha leaped from the car and headed for the pub almost before Maddie had stopped the car. She dashed to the door and stopped to recompose herself. Her heart was still pounding as she fished for her key. Natasha opened the door, her heart stopped and her shoulders sagged as she heard the music.

'Dad's big hit – over-forties only,' she said to the others as they hurried up to her. 'He won't be here now.' With a deep sigh she made her way inside. The others followed apprehensively, listening to the band playing Greg's big Christmas hit, 'When Santa Comes Along'. Natasha looked around the room at all the over-forties tapping, clapping and singing along. She looked disappointed until she noticed Tony leaning back out of one of the booths laughing. She wound her way through the throng and paused before stepping around the screen to say hello. Her face fell when she saw Tony, Julie and Jambo – no sign of Kurt. Jambo pointed to the stage.

Greg came to the end of the song and winced as the guitarist missed a chord. He decided to announce a break, 'But first a special round of applause for this young lad who is playing with us for the first time tonight.' It was then that Greg spotted Natasha, and Natasha and Kurt spotted each other. Feeling in a good mood after the set, Greg unfortunately carried on. 'He's a friend of Natasha's – and if you ask me, if she's looking for a boyfriend she could do a lot worse!'

Kurt turned pale as he sensed any hope he might have with Natasha start to evaporate. He dived across to try to get to the microphone, but too late. Kurt's and Natasha's eyes met and their faces revealed their mutual horror. Natasha was totally embarrassed. She couldn't believe her father had actually stood there and said what she had just heard. Kurt took off the guitar and leapt down from the stage.

'Wait!' he called as Natasha was about to leave.

'How can I? My father likes you!'

Kurt realized this was the kiss of death and watched her walk away.

Chapter 13

By New Year's Eve Kurt and Natasha were
both thoroughly miserable. They had not seen
one another since the Christmas night fiasco
and refused to discuss the evening – or do anything to put things right between them. Kurt's
parents were away and his New Year's Eve
party was going ahead. Kurt had little enthusiasm for it without Natasha – he had not even
invited her, there seemed no point.

Since his parents' departure, the Benson
household had been taken over by varying numbers of young people. At the last minute, as a
special concession and largely because Kurt had
supported them, Lucy and Ollie had been
allowed to stay behind and the house was filled
with their friends as well as Jambo and Tony
who had practically taken up residence. Even
the outside of the house showed signs of the
occupation. Not only was Jambo's car, with
Christmas tree once more in place, parked in
the drive, but Bazz's van was another permanent feature.

After another late night of behaving badly

the only person awake was Jambo. He was installed in front of a roaring fire in the living room reading the newspapers, drinking coffee. This was one of the few tidy rooms in the house. The hall was a mess of discarded coats, boots and shoes and even Ollie looked shocked by the state of the kitchen when he staggered in to make breakfast. He finished by using a mixing bowl and wooden spoon for his Frosties which he was forced to eat standing up.

Hearing movement in the kitchen, Jambo decided it was time for his early morning alarm calls. Pushing Margaret the cow, also holidaying at the Bensons', in front of him, Jambo knocked loudly at Kurt's door. 'Moo-ning campers!' he yelled and frisbeed two pieces of toast into the room at Kurt and Tony. Grinning wickedly as the pair groaned and rolled over, Jambo neatly flicked one soaking wet towel on to Kurt and another on to Tony. By the time they had chased him outside, Jambo had ducked behind Bazz's van.

'You'd better get back inside before you frighten the neighbours,' Jambo laughed. They were both half-dressed.

'You are . . . sick,' Kurt muttered, beginning to notice the cold. 'You are also locked out.'

Jambo was completely unfazed by this and commenced his last alarm call of the morning which entailed rattling the sides of the van and finally throwing up the back sliding panel and blasting a bleary-eyed Bazz with freezing air. Jambo went around to the side of the house, opened the kitchen window and, taking care to leap over the dirty dishes, he climbed back in.

Lucy had now also appeared, looking worn out by her trip downstairs.

'Where's the kettle?' she sighed.

'In the living room – I couldn't face having breakfast in here,' said Jambo.

He then turned to Ollie, 'You and the lot you've got staying in your room can clear up the kitchen, we've got the big party tonight.' In answer to Ollie's protesting look Jambo added, 'You were all in here last night, Lucy and her friends were in the dining room and we were in the living room which is now spotless thanks to yours truly.'

'That's not fair – you wouldn't let us out of the kitchen and you kept coming in to get stuff,' Ollie complained as Kurt and Tony wandered in, closely followed by Bazz. 'And what about them?'

'Tony's on food, Bazz is on music and Kurt'll be useless until we get Nat . . . Nat . . . Natasha here tonight. And please – for all our sakes, if we do get Natasha here, don't let the year end without making a move on her.'

Kurt gave Jambo a look which seemed to question his parentage.

Even the sight of Ollie and his mates struggling to clean the kitchen did nothing to improve Kurt's mood, he hardly listened to anything that was being said and looked as if a black cloud had settled on his shoulders. Finally even Bazz could stand it no longer. He tossed the phone to Kurt, 'Just ask her man . . . just dig the digit.'

'Bazz, look, it's cool. She thinks I'm a prat – fine,' Kurt said.

'So what's changed? She always thought you were a prat!' added Tony.

'I am not going to make it worse by acting like one!'

'Christmas was just . . . one of those things. It's not your fault you're dominated by your mother and weren't allowed out,' Jambo wasn't making things any better. 'Tonight's the best chance you're going to get before your mum and dad get back tomorrow.'

'I am not calling her!'

'Prat!' Jambo, Tony and Bazz chorused in unison. Jambo nodded at the other two and they made a sudden dive on Kurt. In one swift movement they had him locked in their arms and out of the house. They deposited him, still struggling, in the back of Jambo's car where Tony and Bazz effectively sat on him while Jambo drove. Cursing them, Kurt quickly guessed where they were headed.

When they arrived at the Dog in the Pond, Tony, Bazz and Jambo again lifted Kurt and carried him towards the door. This was made more difficult because Kurt was struggling even harder and the three guys kept dissolving into fits of laughter. Finally they made it and set Kurt down.

'That's the hard part done. Now just go in there!' Jambo ordered.

'I've told you, I've made a complete dork of myself over her already and it's time to move on,' Kurt was going to walk away.

The other three barred his path so Kurt was backed up against the door.

'You can't let the year end without reaching the final frontier, man.'

'You've got to boldly go where no Benson has been before . . .'

'You'll thank us for this later.'

And with these words of encouragement they pushed Kurt firmly on the chest so that he was propelled backwards into the pub. He fell crashing and stumbling into the bar and ended up on the floor next to a long pair of legs, belonging to a blonde girl who was not Natasha.

Kurt stood up and struggled to regain his composure as he found himself face to face with the unknown girl. She smiled, instantly attracted.

'And who are you?' Jane Andersen, Natasha's mother asked. She had never met Kurt before.

'Kurt – Kurt Benson.'

'The one Nat's always going on about,' said Sarah, helpfully. Kurt looked pleasantly surprised.

'And what can we do for you, Kurt?' Mrs Andersen asked.

'I . . . came to see Natasha,' Kurt looked acutely embarrassed.

'You're only two thousand miles out then . . .' she explained in answer to Kurt's puzzled look. 'Natasha's in Italy, skiing with her father. Didn't she tell you?'

The other guys looked puzzled and then panic-stricken as Kurt turned to go, his temper smouldering dangerously.

If Kurt had known the full explanation of why Natasha had suddenly decided to go away, he would have felt much better. Natasha had been just as miserable as Kurt for the past few days. In a bid to cheer her up and stop her moping, her parents had tried to persuade her to go with Greg on his annual skiing holiday. At the last minute, she had agreed. It was a bargain that couldn't be refused.

Chapter 14

Dawn spent most of the afternoon talking to her mother. At first there had been the usual awkwardness and stony silences. At one point Dawn had almost stormed off in a huff but something had made her turn back. Her mother was obviously worried and was trying to understand Dawn's feelings. Gradually they began to talk more easily, although Dawn could still not bring herself to answer truthfully her mother's question about whether there was anything else she was not telling her. Finally, Dawn was completely taken aback when her mother offered to postpone marrying Terry for a while to give everyone a chance to think and talk things through properly.

'I'd like that, Mum,' Dawn kissed her mother. 'Are you sure?'

Angela nodded, hugging her daughter. 'I want you to be happy about it all - well, at least comfortable.' Angela held on to Dawn's hand while the two enjoyed their refound intimacy.

'Go on – Louise will be expecting you. Let's face the New Year on a positive note.'

When Dawn arrived at Louise's house she was feeling happier and more relaxed than she had done for a long time. Maddie arrived shortly after her and the three discussed the question of whether or not they should go to Kurt's party – especially with Natasha away. In the end, they decided to go for it.

'And with Nat away . . . I might just make a move on Benson myself!' said Maddie.

'You wouldn't,' Dawn looked surprised.

Maddie hesitated. 'Only to see the New Year in.'

When Maddie rang Kurt's house to invite herself and the others to the party, Dawn was interested to note that Kurt's number was pro-grammed into Maddie's phone.

At the Benson house, party preparations were well under way. Still smarting from the fact that Natasha had gone away without telling him, Kurt was determined to enjoy the party. He took even Jambo by surprise by clicking into gear and taking command of the organization, giving everyone a chore.

'I take it you have recovered from the shock of the skiing Natasha?' Jambo asked.

'If she couldn't be bothered mentioning it . . .' Kurt shrugged and carried on barking out instructions.

Julie and Sarah were at the pub, getting ready to go to the party. When they were about to leave, Jane Andersen looked suspiciously at her daughter, obviously dressed to party and heading for the door, especially as Sarah said 'Bye – see you tomorrow!' She was swiftly called back. Not at all taken in by Sarah's explanation that she was going to stay at Julie's, Jane demanded the truth.

'I'm going to Kurt Benson's party with Julie,' Sarah explained, finally.

At the mention of Kurt's name, the blonde girl at whose feet Kurt had sprawled earlier, looked interested. This was Natasha's cousin, Ruth and she had come to help out at the pub while her uncle was away.

It was at this point that Tony, taking a break from food duty, had walked in. He had decided to surprise Julie by calling for her and he wanted to apologize to Mrs Andersen for what had happened earlier when they had dragged Kurt in. Jane Andersen looked even less keen on the idea of the party. Tony promised to look after both girls and to get them back to Julie's house by one o'clock, but Mrs Andersen was obviously not convinced. Finally Julie whispered something to Tony.

'Would it make you feel better if Ruth came along?' Tony asked.

'But you need me here don't you, Aunt Jane?' Ruth said.

'We usually cope when Greg goes off on one of his gigs and I'd rather have you keeping an eye on Sarah,' Jane replied.

'What about this Benson guy – won't he mind?' Ruth wasn't sure.

'I don't think he'll mind at all,' Tony grinned, looking appraisingly at Ruth.

At Benson's, all was ready and people were beginning to arrive. Jambo appeared, wearing a makeshift headband with a spring of mistletoe on a length of plastic attached to it so that it overhung his head. In answer to Kurt's questioning look Jambo explained, 'It's the JBSH – Jambo Bolton Snogging Helmet. Watch!'

Two girls had just arrived and Jambo stepped in front of them. One of them succumbed to a quick kiss, before giggling her way to the kitchen.

'See?' Jambo looked pleased with himself. 'I could make you one if you like – take your mind off the ice lady.'

'Huh! If she'd rather go skiing with her dad than be here, then it's her hard luck,' Kurt looked momentarily gloomy.

'I knew it was a passing phase – you need someone loyal, dependable and solid. Like Margaret. You'll never catch her skiing,' Jambo tried to cheer Kurt up.

'It's dead – finito . . . no chance . . . no way . . . O.K?'

'You mean can I stop taking the mick?'

'Yes please.'

'Er . . . no!'

The doorbell rang and Tony, Julie, Sarah and

127

Ruth appeared. Jambo and Kurt took one look at another and dashed for the door. Ruth neatly side-stepped the JBSH and Jambo then turned to Julie. Tony stepped protectively in front of her and managed to introduce Ruth before Julie pulled him round towards her. He obviously did not need Jambo's hat. Ruth smiled and walked on into the house. Kurt was about to follow when Jambo pulled him back.

'May I remind you of your affection for her cousin?'

'Er . . . no!'

Bazz had meanwhile spotted Ruth and was trying to introduce himself. 'I'm Bazz. I . . . er . . .'

'Should be doing the music,' Kurt cut in.

'Bazz FM.'

'Britain's loudest!' Ruth said. Bazz looked pleased. 'I saw it on the side of the van – and all the girls at school listen,' Ruth added.

'You're still at school?' Kurt was surprised.

'Sixth form – we have the radio on in the common room. The staff don't even know you're pirate.'

Bazz looked rather offended at this idea.

'It's all that bogus Jungle stuff, Bazz – sad,' Kurt said.

Bazz wandered off to attend to the music, leaving Kurt and Ruth chatting.

'So you don't like Jungle?' Ruth asked.

'Er – do you?' Kurt was unusually cagey, not wanting to blow it.

'Can't stand it . . . Bon Jovi.'

'Early stuff was O.K.'

'Didn't like the cowboy stuff either.'

'So – you're Natasha's cousin,' Kurt said when they had exhausted music.

'Yep – and you're Natasha's . . .'

'Nightmare – I think,' Kurt grinned ruefully. 'We're not an item or anything.'

'But not for want of trying?' Ruth quizzed him.

'And the rest,' Kurt sighed.

'She's always been like that ever since we were kids – she could never decide whether to go on the dodgems or the donkeys,' Ruth sounded sympathetic.

'And what about you?' Kurt stepped closer.

'I'm very definite.'

'Really?'

'Really,' it was now Ruth who moved closer.

Kurt and Ruth stared into each other's eyes, both wondering if the other was serious. They were quickly interrupted by Tony and Julie . . . and Sarah who looked askance at Kurt and Ruth's closeness. Ruth noticed Sarah's expression and felt awkward. Kurt realized and tried to lighten the situation by chatting to Tony about the food but Ruth and Sarah looked at one another in embarrassed silence.

Jambo's next opportunity to try out the JBSH came with the arrival of Maddie, Dawn and Louise.

Maddie, not unexpectedly, told Jambo to drop

dead. Dawn grinned and flicked the mistletoe and was about to walk past when Jambo stopped her.

'Have you ever wondered why we all end up with a draw full of odd socks?' he asked. He looked unfazed as she walked away. He greeted Louise who actually closed her eyes and leant forward to kiss him. Jambo instead walked after Dawn and Ollie stepped into his place, earning himself a slap from Louise when she saw who had kissed her. This left Ollie and his mate Stan in fits of laughter. They were in high spirits and enjoying themselves which is how the disaster in the kitchen occurred.

Along with a few others, Ollie and Stan decided to make a human pyramid on the kitchen table. Unfortunately they collapsed – smashing the table and scattering food everywhere. Lucy, Jambo, Tony and Julie appeared on the scene of devastation seconds later. With Mr and Mrs Benson due back the following day and Kurt's mood unpredictable to say the least, the prospects of Ollie living to enjoy the next year seemed slight, especially as everyone had been warned by Kurt that he wanted no damage or breakages. Taking pity on Ollie's crestfallen face Jambo tried to think of a solution. Julie was sure Tony could solve the problem.

'They have tables like this at college,' Tony commented at last.

'Right!' said Jambo. 'To the college.'

'Wait,' protested Tony. 'You can't, it's not . . .'

'Tony – you're wonderful,' Julie sighed, kissing him. 'I knew you'd think of something.' This left Tony no choice but to assist Jambo in finding a replacement table. Julie was left to pass the word around for everyone to help keep Kurt out of the kitchen.

There was no problem until Kurt saw Ruth leave the room and was about to follow to try to pick up their earlier conversation and intimacy. Dawn, prompted by Julie stepped in to stop him. Suddenly at a loss for something to say Dawn began. 'Er . . . Kurt! Have you ever wondered why we all end up with a drawer full of odd socks?'

Kurt looked bewildered, especially when Dawn, Julie and Louise carried on with this weird topic until Maddie took over and dragged Kurt off to dance. However after a while of this, Kurt excused himself.

'I really do need a drink, Mad,' Kurt headed for the kitchen.

For once Lucy let Ollie persuade her to help him. Kurt was just making his way through the crowd past Ruth when Lucy stopped him.

'We've run out of drink,' she said quickly pulling money from her bag. 'You'll be there and back before anyone else.' Kurt looked a bit suspicious and not at all willing to go. 'I know I can trust you.'

At this, Kurt looked really suspicious. Julie whispered to Ruth who nodded and stepped forward.

'We could get the stuff from the pub if you like,' Ruth suggested. 'I'll go with you.' Kurt was hardly going to refuse now, but there was another awkward moment as he turned to the kitchen for his jacket. Sarah saved the day by appearing in the nick of time with both Kurt's jacket and Ruth's coat. As Ruth and Kurt set off, Tony and Jambo had located a table and were now hoisting it on to the roof of Jambo's car, with the Christmas tree and lights on top of it. All they had to do was secure it tightly.

On the way to and from the pub Kurt and Ruth chatted about school and college, music, what they liked and disliked and what they hoped to do in the future. They had a lot in common and found they laughed at the same things but . . . there was a slight tension between them. They arrived back before Jambo and Tony. Kurt, carrying one box of drink, was set to ask some of the guys to help him bring the rest of the boxes through to the kitchen when Maddie stepped in to divert him.

She grabbed Kurt and gave him a lengthy kiss, which seemed to embarrass Kurt and Ruth. Maddie turned away from Kurt and winked at Ruth who realized Kurt still needed to be kept out of the kitchen. Ruth stepped behind Kurt to stifle a laugh as Maddie cooed, 'We've all missed you.' Kurt looked confused. 'So what did you get?'

'Usual stuff – you know.'

'Show me,' Maddie grabbed his arm. 'I've

never seen it in boxes before.'

'What!?'

'You go and show Maddie – open up the car. I'll get the others to help,' Ruth suggested.

'You serious?' Kurt looked curiously at Maddie for signs of early dementia.

'No. I just wanted us to be alone,' she pulled Kurt towards her but he backed away.

'Look Mad – we had our thing,' Kurt was trying to be nice.

Maddie quickly switched to another topic and asked Kurt probing questions about his mother's choice of Christmas decorations, she then turned to the trimmings on the curtains and finally the wallpaper. Kurt was completely puzzled and didn't have a clue what she was talking about. Even the others who were by now looking on and listening were somewhat surprised at the conversation. Dawn and Louise tried to help out but Kurt's attention had been caught by the lights of a Christmas tree going through the darkened garage.

Jambo and Tony arrived in the kitchen with the table, Christmas tree and lights on top, at the same moment as Kurt – followed by just about everyone else. Kurt took in the scene and with one swift move, grabbed Ollie.

'Well?!' Kurt asked.

'We got a replacement,' Ollie said, preparing to die.

'Almost,' Jambo pointed out. He held up a piece of the old table against the new. It was the same, but a different colour and varnish.

'You picked up the wrong one, dog brain!' Ollie yelled.

'It was dark,' Tony protested. Julie hugged him defensively.

'You're one big accident aren't you, Ollie?' something in Kurt's tone told Ollie that this was the time to disappear. He wriggled free and away out of the door. Kurt followed.

'You have to come home some time, Ollie!' Kurt called from the front door. As the others came out, Kurt grabbed Tony and Jambo. 'And you two back to college – with a torch this time. I do not want to have to explain things to "serial mom" tomorrow!' Kurt pushed Jambo and Tony back into the house to find a torch.

'Is your mother that bad?' Ruth asked.

Kurt grinned and shrugged. 'I'm sure we'll cope,' he checked his watch. 'It won't be long till midnight and we are forced together by the customary New Year kiss,' he moved closer.

'I don't think so, do you?' Ruth said, a touch wistfully.

'So it was all just a decoy, then?'

'Not all of it,' Ruth looked at Kurt and his face brightened. 'But there is Natasha to think about,' Ruth paused. 'I think I should go and help out back at the pub. I'll only get in the way otherwise and I don't want to do that . . . or make a fool of myself.'

Kurt nodded and they held each other's gaze

for a moment knowing that what stood between them was Natasha.

'Some other time then,' Kurt smiled.

'Perhaps . . . tell Sarah I'll say she's at Julie's.'

Kurt watched Ruth go, wondering what might have been. One thing he was sure of as the New Year loomed – he had to sort things out with Natasha, properly, once and for all.

The crowd that had gathered on the steps and in the hall was dispersing. Jambo turned and saw Tony and Julie lost in each other again. He raised his eyes to the heavens and saw Dawn doing the same thing. They both grinned. Dawn pointed at his sweatshirt and the equation printed on the front – 10 + 10 = 10.

'What's that?' she asked.

'The number of atoms in the human body – one plus one equals one . . . but it takes some practice,' he explained. Dawn laughed. Jambo bobbed his JBSH in front of her and smiling, she was about to step forward. Jambo was also left to wonder what might have been as Kurt chose this instant to yank him backwards towards his car.

When midnight struck, Tony and Jambo wished one another Happy New Year as they headed back to college.

SAPLING ORDER FORM

Beverley Hills:
- ☐ 1 85283 675 X   Factfile   £4.99 pb
- ☐ 1 85283 671 7   French Rival   £2.99 pb
- ☐ 1 85283 816 7   Two Hearts   £2.99 pb
- ☐ 1 85283 821 3   Where the Boys Are   £2.99 pb
- ☐ 1 85283 749 7   Which Way to the Beach?   £2.99 pb

Blossom:
- ☐ 0 7522 0926 4   Family Album   £3.99 pb
- ☐ 0 7522 0931 0   Trouble with Secrets   £2.99 pb

California Dreams:
- ☐ 0 7522 0906 X   Perfect Harmony   £3.50 pb
- ☐ 0 7522 0916 7   Playing for Keeps   £3.50 pb
- ☐ 0 7522 0911 6   Who Can You Trust   £3.50 pb

Hollyoaks:
- ☐ 0 7522 0150 6   Can't Get the Girl   £3.99 pb
- ☐ 0 7522 0145 X   Coming Together   £3.99 pb

Saved By The Bell:
- ☐ 0 7522 0623 0   Bayside Madness   £3.50 pb
- ☐ 0 7522 0618 4   California Scheming   £3.50 pb
- ☐ 0 7522 0196 4   Computer Confusion   £3.50 pb
- ☐ 0 7522 0191 3   Don't Tell a Soul   £3.50 pb
- ☐ 0 7522 0901 9   Girl's Night Out   £3.50 pb
- ☐ 0 7522 0181 6   Impeach Screech   £3.50 pb
- ☐ 0 7522 0608 7   Kelly's Hero   £3.50 pb
- ☐ 0 7522 0613 3   Ol' Zack Magic   £3.50 pb
- ☐ 0 7522 0995 7   One Wild Weekend   £3.50 pb
- ☐ 0 7522 0186 7   Silver Spurs   £3.50 pb
- ☐ 0 7522 0990 6   Zack's Last Scam   £3.50 pb
- ☐ 0 7522 0985 X   Zack Strikes Back   £3.50 pb

Saved By The Bell – New Class:
- ☐ 0 7522 0670 2   Breaking the Rules   £3.50 pb
- ☐ 0 7522 0665 6   Going, Going, Gone   £3.50 pb
- ☐ 0 7522 0660 5   Spilling the Beans   £3.50 pb
- ☐ 0 7522 0655 9   Trouble Ahead   £3.50 pb

Tear Jerkers:
- ☐ 0 7522 0246 4   Family Secrets   £2.99 pb
- ☐ 0 7522 0251 0   Once in a Blue Moon   £2.99 pb
- ☐ 0 7522 0241 3   Remember Me   £2.99 pb
- ☐ 0 7522 0236 7   Runaway   £2.99 pb

All these books are available at your local bookshop or can be ordered direct from the publisher. Just tick the titles you want and fill in the form below.

Prices and availability subject to change without notice.

Boxtree Cash Sales, P.O. Box 11, Falmouth, Cornwall TR10 9EN

Please send a cheque or postal order for the value of the book and add the following for postage and packing:

U.K. including B.F.P.O. – £1.00 for one book plus 50p for the second book, and 30p for each additional book ordered up to a £3.00 maximum.

Overseas including Eire – £2.00 for the first book plus £1.00 for the second book, and 50p for each additional book ordered.

OR please debit this amount from my Access/Visa Card (delete as appropriate).

Card Number   ☐☐☐☐☐☐☐☐☐☐☐☐☐☐☐☐

Amount £ ....

Expiry Date ....

Signed ....

Name ....

Address ....